Say Something

by Jennifer L. Allen

Say Something
Copyright © 2018 Jennifer L. Allen

Published: Jennifer L. Allen 2018
jennifer@jenniferlallenauthor.com
Editor: Aimee Lukas
Cover Design: Cover Me, Darling

Dedication

To anyone who has ever experienced infertility...
You are not alone.
You are not less than.
You are enough.

To my husband...
Thank you for always being my biggest fan,
~~Even~~ Especially when I didn't feel like I was
worth it.

Author's Note

This book touches on something that far too many couples suffer in silence about. Infertility. It's amazing how many people you know have experienced it to some degree once you start talking about it. I struggled with infertility years ago, and after a year of trying to conceive, I finally had some tests done and learned that I had to have my fallopian tubes removed, a partial hysterectomy, just like Jessica in the story. If I hadn't gotten breast cancer, IVF probably would have been an option for my husband and I, but it's off the table now. Adoption is the way we'll go when we're ready, and that's okay. We always talked about adopting, even when we thought we could have our own biological kids. Our experience with infertility kind of reinforced the idea that adopting was what we were meant to do, you know? I took some liberties with the storyline here, since I didn't experience everything my characters did, but some of what they went through—what they felt—was directly from my own experiences. If there's anyone out there who is experiencing or has experienced infertility, I just wanted to write this note to let you know that you are not alone. It may still be a taboo subject for much of society, but it's absolutely not something to be ashamed of. You are not less than because of this, you are more than enough. We are enough. <3

I steered my car down the two lane, one-stoplight street that bisected my hometown of Oak River. The small town was aptly named for both the tall trees that lined nearly all its roads and the river that was nestled behind the properties on the north side of Main Street. I hadn't been back for years, yet nothing seemed to have changed. If anything, it was greener, the lush landscape having filled in even more.

I never thought returning to Oak River to live was something that was in the cards for me. Don't get me wrong, I loved my small hometown, but I'd always imagined bigger and better things for myself. I guess I'd envisioned a lot of things for myself that never happened.

Turning onto Maple Lane, I passed by the Law Office of George A. Smith, right on the corner, soon to be the Law Office of Jessica L. Price. I smiled at the thought...at the *promise* for my future. A new beginning in an old, familiar place.

I reflected on all that had transpired over the past month. Buying the practice from Mr.

Smith, quitting my job at a corporate law firm, and packing up my entire life to relocate back to the place I'd grown up. Stranger things had happened.

Three minutes and a few turns later, I was pulling into the long cobblestoned driveway of my parents' Tudor-style home. The massive home was tucked back in the trees, and it took half a minute of riding down the driveway before it came into view. I had just shifted the car into park when my mother came running out the front door, her dark blonde hair, identical to mine, flowing behind her.

"My baby is home!"

I put on my best smile, pushed open the door and hopped out of the car. "Mom!"

She embraced me in a way only a mother could and for the first time since everything went so terribly wrong, I cried in my mother's arms. I unloaded the burden of not being able to have a baby. I let go of the memory of Danny walking out the front door of our home nearly four years ago, officially slamming the door shut on our marriage—our future. I cried.

"Oh, baby. Don't cry, don't cry," she soothed, running her fingers through my long hair the way she had when I was a child. "You're so brave. So brave for doing this. I'm so proud of you. You're going to do so well here. Everyone in town is excited to have you back. They're proud of you, too. One of our own becoming a big shot lawyer."

I laughed through my tears. "A big shot lawyer?" Hardly. I'd been at the bottom of the totem pole at the corporate law office I'd worked at prior to moving home. I basically proofread contracts that were put together by the other attorneys. *Big shot* was not how I'd choose to describe myself. But I couldn't complain. It had been an easy, brainless job with a ridiculous salary that afforded me the ability to purchase the practice here in Oak River and not live off ramen noodles while I waited for the business to prosper.

My mother pulled away and framed my face in her hands. "Not at that place in the city," she said "city" with distaste—my mom loved small town life and couldn't understand why anyone in their right mind would want to live amongst so many skyscrapers and exhaust fumes. "Here in Oak River. You're not even thirty yet, and you own your own practice! You're a big shot to us simple folk."

I smiled genuinely, my chest filling up with pride. My mother was right, though I'd disagree that there was anything *simple* about the people of Oak River, but I did have a lot to be proud of. I *was* a big shot, in my own right.

"Let's get your stuff inside. Everyone's coming over for dinner tonight to welcome you back."

I paused on my way to retrieve my overnight bag from the trunk and glanced at my mother. "Everyone?" I asked, raising an eyebrow.

"The family," my mom said. "Melissa, Michael, Bryan, Karla, and the kids."

My smile was back. I couldn't wait to see my brothers and sister. And my nephews and niece...I hadn't even met the youngest, Evan, and he was three years old now. I should be

3

ashamed...but being around babies—around someone who was pregnant—at that dark time in my life had been difficult. I wasn't in a good place. It was never that I wasn't happy for my brother and his wife—I was. I loved them both so much and they deserved every happiness bestowed upon them, children included. I'd never wish them anything other than the best. It was the reminder that my body was defective that hurt me so much.

I only hoped they'd understand. I hoped they'd forgive me.

I walked across the lawn towards the front door and caught a glimpse of the old latticed archway in the garden on the side of the house. Memories of a happier time came rushing back.

Feeling like a princess high up in a tower, I looked through the window of my childhood bedroom, out into the yard full of family and friends. The sun was shining and there wasn't a cloud in the bright blue sky, it was a beautiful day. My parents garden was the perfect, colorful backdrop for our big day. Mom's flowers had bloomed in bright reds and pinks, bold oranges, and luscious violets. She'd planted them all earlier in the season with my special day in mind. Deep green ivy climbed the lattice of the archway Danny and I were getting married under in a little while. It was picture perfect.

Moving my gaze a little to the left, I watched Danny interact with his groomsmen, which included his brother, Dean, as his best man, and my brothers Bryan and Michael. I know I wasn't supposed to see him, but how could I resist? He was so handsome in his tux. He looked so confident, too, like there was absolutely no question in his mind that he was where he was meant to be in that very moment. I felt the same way.

Just as I watched my father approach Danny and wrap him in a fatherly embrace, a knock sounded on the door.

"You decent?" my sister, Melissa, called out.

"As if you care," Karla, my sister-in-law commented as Melissa pushed open the door, not waiting for a reply from me.

I smiled as my family poured in the room. Behind Melissa and Karla was my mom, Danny's mom, and Danny's sister, Darcy. The three girls, dressed in identical lilac knee-length gowns, made up my bridal party. My mom and Danny's each chose a different peridot ensemble.

"Oh, you look beautiful," Mrs. Thompson said as she entered the room. She went straight to the bed and picked up my veil. She had done my hair earlier in the day but was waiting until after I was dressed to attach the veil. "Danny is going to be beside himself."

"There won't be a dry eye anywhere," Mom confirmed.

"Were you peeking?" Melissa teased, looking out the window at the small congregation.

I shrugged. "I may have checked things out."

"Tsk tsk," Karla chided.

"You look great, Darce," I told Danny's younger sister. She was always very quiet around us, and probably would have preferred to have been anywhere but there, but she was family so she was right where she belonged, whether she realized it or not.

"Thanks," she mumbled. At least I thought that's what she said.

"Are you nervous?" Melissa asked.

"Are you excited?" Karla elbowed Melissa.

I laughed. I'd missed those two while I was away at school. "I'm not nervous at all," I answered, turning to them after Mrs. T had finished adjusting my veil. "It feels so right."

"Aww," they said together.

"You guys are the perfect couple," Melissa added.

"You make my son so happy, Jessica," Mrs. T told me.

"He makes me so happy."

Mrs. T went into her purse and pulled out a small jewelry box. "If you haven't already picked out earrings for today, I'd love it if you'd wear these. They were my mother's. She wore them on her wedding day, I wore them on mine, and I'd love it if you'd wear them on yours."

I opened the box and nestled in a little cloud of cotton were a simple pair of diamond stud earrings. They were more beautiful than anything I had in my jewelry box. "I'd love to wear them."

"I had them cleaned," she said, removing them from the box and handing them to me.

I put the studs in my ears and looked at my reflection. Mrs. T appeared behind me and placed her hand on my shoulder. "They're gorgeous," I said.

"You're gorgeous. I already considered you a part of our family, but after today it will be official."

Tears welled in my eyes as I placed my hand over hers. This moment was so special to me. I smiled at our reflection and took a deep breath. In just a short while, I'd officially be a Thompson.

My life couldn't possibly get any better.

***

"Did mom tell you?" my sister, Melissa, asked later that night.

It turned out I had nothing to worry about. The entire Price brood had welcomed me back into their lives and their hearts with open arms. My younger brother Michael had been a little standoffish, but overall, I'd call my first family dinner in several years a success. The kids asked me all sorts of questions about living in the city. I even fielded a few questions from my nephews about whether I'd ever met any superheroes. Sadly the answer to that question was no, even though I could have used a little Captain America in my life. Or the actor who played him. Or Thor. Really, I wasn't picky. Any of the Avengers would have done just fine.

"Tell me what?" I asked, handing her a dripping wet dish to dry. I picked up another dirty plate to scrub.

"Danny's back."

I dropped the dish I was holding. It bounced off the edge of the counter, narrowly missing the sink, and crashed to the floor, shattering to pieces at our bare feet. The room went deathly silent, save for the ringing in my ears and the echo of the broken plate.

Danny's back.

"Don't move," my father said from the doorway, setting down the casserole dish he was carrying in from the dining room. He moved to grab the broom and dustpan from the mudroom off the kitchen and returned to the kitchen to start sweeping.

"Everything okay?" my mother asked, walking into the kitchen. "I heard something break." Bryan and Karla had left with the kids about thirty minutes before, and Dad and Michael were clearing the table while Melissa and I washed the dishes. Mom had been relaxing in the living room, sticking to the motto that *the cook never cleans.*

"Just a plate, dear," my father answered, still sweeping up the mess.

I hadn't moved, still frozen in place over the sink, staring blankly out the window into the backyard. Melissa looked at me with a concerned expression. "You okay?" she whispered.

I snapped out of my fog, nodding. I even offered her a poor attempt at a smile, but she could read right through it. It's one of the reasons I had stayed away over the years. I was so transparent. My family could always see right through me. There would have been no hiding my torment. My sorrow. And I didn't want the pity...I couldn't handle the pity.

"I'm sorry. I shouldn't have sprung it on you like that."

"It's okay," I said, placing my hand on her arm and stopping her from saying anything else. "Just caught me by surprise."

Danny.

Danny Thompson.

My high school sweetheart.

My first love...my first everything.

My ex-husband, whom I hadn't seen in years, just happened to be back in the same small town as me. Why? How? *When?* I had so many questions. None of which I even had the right to ask anymore. What Danny did was no longer any of my business.

"We'll talk later," Melissa said, not entirely letting me off the hook but giving me some reprieve in the presence of our parents. I rolled my eyes but nodded at my persistent sister.

Why couldn't I catch a break?

The evening had been so peaceful...so wonderful. I enjoyed spending time with my parents and reconnecting with my siblings and the kids; they accepted me right into the fold. Turns out my brother and his wife talked about their "auntie in the city" with them all the time, so they felt like they knew me already. For the first time in a long time, I had felt like I was somewhere I belonged. Like everything might have finally been okay.

Why did the bottom always have to drop out?

2

"Want to talk about it?" Melissa asked once we'd said goodnight to mom and dad and retired to our shared childhood bedroom. There were plenty of rooms in the house, but Melissa and I had always shared a room, even when we grew out of it. She had a house on the other side of town, but she insisted on spending my first night back in Oak River with me. She was truly the best sister. The better sister.

Younger than me by one year, Melissa had followed in our father's footsteps and gone to college for journalism. Our family had owned the local newspaper for generations, and she was currently a staff reporter. I was sure that when Dad eventually retired, she would take his place as Editor in Chief. She would have earned it, too, having started out on the bottom rung of the ladder as a clerk, running errands for anyone who needed anything. She'd fallen in love with the hustle and bustle of the newsroom back then—as much as Oak Ridge hustled and bustled—and I wasn't surprised when she'd chosen it for her career.

"I was just surprised to hear his name," I told her the partial truth. Sure, I hadn't heard Danny's name spoken aloud since our divorce proceedings, but it wasn't his name that shocked me. It was the fact that he was *here,* in Oak River. He'd wanted to get out of here as badly as I had, more so even. He had his sights set on big things, like coaching college football somewhere amazing.

We'd had so many dreams back then...our whole lives ahead of us.

"Surprised he's back?"

"Yeah," I admitted, burrowing further under the covers of my old twin bed.

"I heard he's coaching at the high school."

I loved my sister...I missed her...but I really wished she'd stop talking. It was hard enough for me to stop thinking about Danny on a good day, never mind after having this bomb dropped on me. What were the chances he and I would both end up back home at the same time? Some would have said it was fate bringing us back together...kismet. I didn't know about all that. I thought it was simply a coincidence. Not even a purely random coincidence since this was where our families were.

"That's nice," I responded, knowing I wouldn't get away with not acknowledging her.

"Is it?" she asked.

"Sure," I said, and I meant it. I didn't wish any harm on Danny. Quite the opposite. I just wasn't ready to bump into him around town. I thought I'd have a few more years before running into him, *if ever.* It took a long time (and a lot of therapy) to bring me back to the land of the living, and that was in a world where Danny no longer existed. Now we existed again in the same place, and I wasn't quite sure how I felt about that.

"I also hear he's still single."

I let out a sigh. Having a journalist for a sister was *so much fun*. Maybe if I ignored her now, she'd think I was asleep and shut up.

"He's renovating his uncle's old place."

Maybe not.

"Melissa!"

"What?"

"Can we please go to sleep? I had a long drive today. I'm tired. And I don't want to talk about my ex-husband."

Now it was her turn to sigh. "Whatever. We'll talk tomorrow when you're less cranky." Her bed creaked as she turned over; just like it had when we were kids; it brought me an odd sense of peace as the blankets rustled and then quieted.

"Not likely," I muttered under my breath, not quite ready to let her have the final word.

"Oh, it's happening, sister. I've given you years of peace and quiet. Time's up."

I rolled onto my back again and stared up at the ceiling. Melissa wouldn't relent. I knew that. I'd be facing the music sooner or later. Might as well have been sooner.

My family had given me space after the divorce. Mostly because I'd stopped speaking to them long before then, and they'd gotten tired of being ignored or hung up on. After weeks of their calls being sent to voicemail, emails unreturned, and knocks unanswered...they finally stopped trying. Not that I could blame them. They knew I was alive, I'd sent out the bare minimum, "I'm okay" texts, and I was sure Danny updated them before we divorced. So there was really nothing left for my family to do but wait. I guess they'd had faith that I'd come around.

Eventually I made contact and apologized for distancing myself, but it took a while for things to get back to normal...or to a new normal, rather. And even so, our relationship was still long distance. They forgave me, because that's what family did. They forgave you for your moments of weakness and selfishness and helped you move forward. That's what I was supposed to be doing here in Oak River. Moving forward.

But now a big piece of my past was back, and I didn't know how to handle that.

"I can't believe you guys get to work on a farm all summer," I said, taking in the wide open space that was Danny and Dean's Uncle Pete's farm. It never ceased to amaze me that there was property like this just outside the suburban streets of Oak River.

"It's not all it's cracked up to be," Dean whined. "Farm work is tough."

I had no doubt about that. The massive barn housed several horses and there were also chickens. Uncle Pete had some crops, too. Corn and wheat. I didn't know what went into running a farm, but if their uncle needed the help of his nephews and my brothers, I imagined it was a lot of work.

"We should go to the river and go swimming after this," Danny suggested. I watched a drop of sweat fall from his brow to his bare chest, then run all the way down until it was absorbed by his pants.

Lately, whenever I was around Danny, I felt weird. My hands got sweaty, my head felt fuzzy and my heart pounded...like when I have to give a presentation at school. I'd known Danny all my life, why was I suddenly nervous around him.

"Swimming sounds fun," Melissa said. She pulled a small nail file out of her purse and started filing her nails. My sister was so bored. Aside from swimming or laying out in the sun to get tanned, she didn't care much for being outside.

"I wouldn't mind cooling off after this," Dean agreed.

"We'd better get back to work so we'll have time to cool off before it gets dark," Bryan said, wiping the sweat off his brow before he replaced his baseball cap.

The boys all got up and left the porch, Mikey trailing behind them. My younger brother hated manual labor. I was surprised anyone had convinced him to help out, but I'd bet Mom and Dad didn't give him a choice. Our family was close with the Thompsons, and when either family needed help, the other pitched in.

I watched Danny's back, as he moved with the others across the field. I'd always thought he was handsome, but he was just a friend, right? Our parents were very close, so we always played with each other when we were younger. We were also in the same classes throughout elementary and middle school, since our small town only had one class per grade. High school would start in the fall, ninth grade, and I wasn't sure what that would bring since it would be the first time we took classes with other grades. We hadn't gotten our schedules yet, but I was hoping Danny and I would have some of the same classes.

I flipped through the latest issue of YM magazine while Melissa did her nails beside me. I started to feel bad for just sitting on the porch swing with my sister while the guys were out working hard in the sticky heat.

"Do you want to go help them?"

Melissa gave me a side-eye as she did her second coat of Wet n Wild hot pink nail polish. "Why would I do that? My nails will get all messed up."

"I don't know."

"You just want to go see Danny. Admit it."

My cheeks heated. "I do not."

Melissa smirked as she stuck the brush back in the bottle and sealed it. She waved her hands back and forth in front of her, causing the swing to sway. "There's nothing wrong if you like him, you know?"

"I don't like him." I liked him as a friend, but that was it, I thought.

"Uh huh." I wanted to wipe that smirk off her face. Sometimes I wondered why my sister was my best friend. She dropped her polish and file into her tote bag and stood up. "Okay, let's go."

"Go where?"

"To find the guys."

"We don't have to," I said.

"Okay, then let's stay here."

I stood up. "Okay, come on."

Melissa laughed, then carefully took my hand as we skipped off the porch.

"Are you going to try out for cheerleading?" Melissa asked as we walked through the field to where the boys were fixing a fence.

"Why would I do that?" I didn't think I was coordinated enough to be a cheerleader.

"I overhead Danny talking to Bryan. He's trying out for JV football."

"Really?"

"Yup. And the cheerleaders get to go to all the games with the football team."

"They do?"

"Yup. I'll help you practice, if you want."

"Thanks," I said.

Melissa may have been my younger sister...but I guess she was a pretty amazing best friend, too.

***

My mother made a huge breakfast the next morning, and as I made my plate I absently wondered if half the reason she cooked all the time was so she didn't have to clean up afterwards. It seemed she dirtied every single pot, pan, and utensil in the kitchen, but I wouldn't complain...at least not out loud. Her breakfast buffet of pancakes, eggs, bacon, sausage, and fresh fruit was to die for, and I needed to get my fill before I was on my own in my new place. If that meant I had to spend the next week washing dishes, I would happily comply.

"Melissa said she told you about Danny," Mom said as she poured orange juice into my glass.

Damn you, Melissa, I silently cursed my sister. The little brat left early and rode with my dad to the office, leaving me alone with our mom and the dishes. It was just like Melissa to do something like that.

"Mm-hmm," I acknowledged, hoping she didn't press any further, but knowing it wasn't likely.

"I didn't know he was coming back," she told me, placing her hand gently on mine. I released the white-knuckle grip I had on my fork, not realizing I'd been squeezing it so tight.

"It's okay, Mom," I said. "We were bound to cross paths again at some point with me being back here." Realistically, I knew that. His parents still lived here, after all. He wasn't the terrible, estranged child I was. He probably came back to visit his parents and siblings over the years after we split up. After all, there had been numerous trips back home while we were married that I bailed on for one made up reason or another.

Mom gave me sad smile and squeezed my shoulder. "If you ever want to talk about anything, I'm here for you, sweetheart."

"Thanks, Mom," I said, looking down at my plate so she couldn't see my eyes well up with tears.

She had no idea how much I wished I'd confided in her when my life was falling apart. I was too proud back then. I had wanted to show her and my dad that I was independent and that I could make it on my own and be an adult. Running home to my mom after too many disheartening doctors' appointments and too many failed infertility treatments would have felt too much like admitting defeat. I was never ready or willing to admit that, even though I had been so utterly defeated. I was such an *idiot*. If there was one thing I had learned over the years, it was that one of the most crucial parts of adulthood was recognizing and then admitting when you needed help.

"What's on your agenda for today?" she asked, and I was thankful for the change in topic.

"I'm going to run by the practice and check on the house. I need to see what needs to be done before the movers show up next week."

"You'll probably want to paint. I don't imagine Mr. Smith has updated much in that old house. He had a few tenants, so who knows what condition it's in."

Thanks, Mom. I feel so much better now.

The "house" was actually a small cottage set behind Mr. Smith's law practice. When I bought the practice, the home came with it. It seemed like the perfect new start, at least temporarily. Mr. and Mrs. Smith never lived in the house; they'd been renting it out until a few years ago. It was all sight unseen, and I hoped I didn't end up with a complete lemon on my hands. I had a lot of hope riding on a relatively easy move-in transition. With my mother's words, I was beginning to feel uneasy about the whole thing.

"I'll probably need to air it out, too," I said, my mind conjuring up the old, musty odor that was likely to be behind closed doors.

"Why don't we make a day of it?" Mom asked, her eyes brightening up. "We can do a walk through, then hit the hardware store for supplies."

Her excitement was contagious, and I loved that she wanted to be involved. Some of my dread lifted. I couldn't think of a better way to spend my day than getting my new home ready with my mom.

3

"It could be worse," Mom said.

"Please," I stated dryly, my hands perched on my hips, "enlighten me on how this could possibly be any worse?"

"It has a roof."

I looked up at the white, popcorn ceiling stained with water marks. "Barely," I scoffed.

"There could be no electricity or running water..."

I walked over to the kitchen sink and turned on the tap. The pipes groaned, but nothing came out. I sighed as my stomach knotted. "Any other words of wisdom?"

"The water is probably turned off," she shrugged. "I'm sorry, sweetie."

We stood in the kitchen of the small, nine hundred square foot cottage, a.k.a. disaster area, and I scanned the space. As much as I hated to admit it, my mother was right. It could have been worse. The once white carpet in the living area and bedroom was mostly brown. The linoleum in the kitchen and bathroom was worn through in several places. There were holes in the walls from who knew what—it looked like something chewed through in a few places—as well as several broken windows that were being held together with masking tape. But at least it was still standing. Silver linings and all that.

"I'm going to need to hire someone," I muttered to myself. This was more than a quick paint job.

Mom started clapping her hands excitedly, and I raised an eyebrow at her. "You can use Michael!"

"Michael? As in my brother? Your son, Michael?" My tone must have indicated my surprise because she rolled her eyes at me.

"Of course, what other Michael would I recommend?"

"I don't know..." I started, biting my lip. The Michael I remembered wasn't a handy guy. He had been a bookworm all through high school. Could he really repair a house? I knew from our conversation over dinner last night that he was working in construction, but I kind of figured he did paperwork or something.

"What's there to think about? He's your brother."

"He'll probably write messages in glow-in-the-dark paint throughout the house to scare the hell out of me, Mom."

She smiled, probably remembering the time he'd rearranged the glow-in-the-dark stars on mine and Melissa's bedroom ceiling to make spiders and scary faces. We didn't sleep in our room for a week after that. "He takes his work very seriously, Jess. He'd do a good job for you."

"I'll give him a call."

21

"I think that'd make him very happy." She squeezed my shoulder before stepping around me and heading out the door. "Call him now, then we'll go look at paint swatches and get some lunch."

I pulled my cell phone out of my pocket and skimmed the contacts for Michael's number, then tapped his name and waited for the call to connect.

"Michael Price," he answered, and I smiled at how professional my little brother sounded.

"Hey, Mikey. It's Jess."

He was quiet for a moment before responding. "Hey, Jess. What's up?"

Guilt ate at me. Talking to my little brother on the phone shouldn't have been awkward. He was my brother. We hadn't spoken much at dinner the night before, but we had exchanged some pleasantries. Nevertheless, there was a strain there.

"Mom and I are at my new place," I told him. "It needs some work."

"I'm pretty busy today," he started, and I interrupted him; I knew I shouldn't have asked.

"It's okay. I'm sorry to have bothered you. Maybe you can recommend someone?"

"Jess, stop. If you'll let me finish...I'm busy today, but I can probably meet you there tomorrow morning to check things out."

I blew out a relieved breath, some of the tension left my shoulders. "Really?"

"Of course," he said assuredly. "I'll see you in the morning."

"Thanks, Mike."

"No problem."

I told him goodbye, disconnected the call, and tucked my phone back in my pocket. For the first time since walking in the house and seeing the damage, I felt like everything was going to be okay. I took one final look around the small, open floor plan and smiled, imagining its potential.

Things would come together.

They just had to. There wasn't any other option.

***

"I really liked that shade of brown you picked out for your bedroom," Mom said as she stirred the sugar into her iced tea. She always used to complain that restaurants couldn't get the sugar to tea ratio quite right, and it appeared she still held that opinion. At least she developed her own solution to the problem.

"I love the color," I responded, leaving out the fact it was the exact same color Danny and I had painted the bedroom of our townhome in the city. I wasn't happy to admit it, but I'd never had them out to visit the townhouse, so she wouldn't know how the place was decorated. Life had been too busy with college and work; it was just easier for Danny and me to go home for holidays and quick visits. Not to mention that things went south so quickly after we'd moved in, and I'd begun to distance myself from everyone. The only person who would recognize the color was Danny...and he'd never see it. It wasn't like he had any reason to be in my bedroom.

"I can't wait to see what Michael does with the place," she said excitedly before biting into her grilled chicken wrap.

"There's not much to do," I said to her. "Just the ceiling, walls, windows, and flooring." You know...just everywhere you looked. Our eyes met, and we burst out laughing at the absurdity of my statement. There was *so* much to do.

"You'd be surprised what a difference just those things will make," Mom said after we'd composed ourselves.

I nodded, taking a forkful of my Caesar salad. She was right. The interior of the house looked like an abandoned shack. It smelled like one, too. But once the aesthetics were taken care of, the cottage would look like a whole new place. Not to mention what a difference adding splashes of color would make.

As we continued to eat in silence, I realized how much I'd missed The Diner. Yes, that's what it was called: *The Diner*. It was the only diner in Oak River, so it was suitably named. We—Danny and I—used to come here after school on the days we didn't have practice or some club meeting. In fact, the last time I was here was the last day of our final summer in Oak River before we left for college—almost twelve years ago. I'd gotten a strawberry milkshake and he had a root beer float. Everything about the place was comfortable and homey, from the rich and delicious comfort foods to the super sweet desserts.

"How long do you think the repairs will take?" I asked my mom, remembering they had

24

some renovations done to their kitchen a few years back.

"I guess it depends on when he could fit you in and if he has to order the materials. I don't think the work itself will take that long. The cottage isn't that big."

I nodded. That was good. As happy as I was to be spending time with my family, I'd been living on my own for so long that I really liked having my own space. Not to mention, the movers were coming soon. I didn't want to have to postpone the delivery of my stuff. Not that it was much, I could probably stow it in my parents' basement or garage.

"You know you're more than welcome to stay with us as long as you need," Mom said, reading my mind.

I smiled at her from across the booth. "I know, Mom. I appreciate that. I was just thinking about the movers. They'll be here next week and I'm hoping I have a place for them to deliver my stuff."

"Just talk to Michael, I'm sure he'll do everything he can to get it done on time for you."

I hoped that was the case, but I wasn't so sure. Things between Michael and I felt off, but I didn't dare tell my mother that. She would have called him up right then and there and tried to fix whatever was broken, and I wasn't entirely sure anything was broken. I just didn't really know my brother anymore. He was in high school when I left, and now he was all grown up. We used to talk on the phone a lot, but that stopped when everything in my life started to go wrong.

"I will. I didn't realize his company did residential work." At dinner, he had said his company did commercial construction, which is why I hadn't even thought to ask him for help with the house. That and the fact that I figured he was an inspector or something, not an actual construction laborer.

"They don't, but you're his sister."

"I haven't been much of one," I said before I could stop myself.

Mom looked at me with a frown on her face. "Your brothers and sister don't feel that way, you know? None of us do. We know you went through some really difficult things and that you needed time."

"I completely blocked all of you out, Mom. On purpose." I added quietly, looking out the large, plate glass window of the diner. I avoided eye contact, not wanting to see the pity in her eyes. There was always pity in people's eyes when they'd learned of my struggles. Pity and discomfort because people rarely knew what to say. It was as though infertility was the equivalent to leprosy for some people. Not that I ever really wanted to talk about it, but maybe I would have if the reception wasn't so avoidant.

A familiar blue pickup truck moved down Main Street, and my heart started racing.

No, it couldn't be. Not today. I wasn't ready to see him. Not this soon.

The truck kept going, passing the diner, and I sighed in relief.

My mom reached across the table and took my hand. I pulled my gaze from the window and looked into her dark, understanding eyes, so like my own. "We forgive you."

"Thanks, Mom," I said, offering a smile. "I'm sorry I'm not much fun today."

"Pish posh," she said, waving her hand in dismissal. "You're my daughter. Spending time with you is always fun."

Her words made me feel lighter and comfortable. I couldn't help but wonder how different my life could have been had I just reached out to my mother when everything was falling apart.

Would Danny and I still be together?

Would I have still lost all those years to the darkness?

"I'm sure you thought that very thing when Melissa and I were tearing up the formal gown section of the department store when we were kids." Melissa and I had a thing for the fancy dresses when we were way too young to wear them, but that never stopped us from running away from our mom at the mall and playing amongst the silk and satin.

"Oh, lord no. I didn't start enjoying spend time with you hellions until you got a bit older," she said, and we laughed together.

As I took a sip of my tea, still contemplating some of life's big questions, my mom's eyes widened at something behind me.

4

I swear I could feel his presence before he spoke a single word. My skin prickled with awareness, hairs stood on end...my blood came alive. My entire being was humming with an energy only Danny could generate. I hadn't heard his voice—seen his face—in three years, yet the connection was still there as if it were yesterday. We'd been invisibly tethered to one another since we were sixteen years old.

Frozen in place, I was unsure of what to do. I wasn't prepared for this...wasn't prepared to fully consider us being in the same town again, let alone the same room—the same diner—that held so many of our young memories. They were good, innocent memories, before adult stuff got the best of us.

Well, I couldn't exactly run away from him. Not only would that have been childish, but it was also impossible since he'd moved into my peripheral and was now blocking my escape route from the booth. It was either crash through the window, or him. Neither was an appealing option.

My wide eyes were focused on my mother, the straw from my glass of iced tea still between my puckered lips.

Mom smiled at me reassuringly and stood up. "It's good to see you, Danny," she said, pulling him in for a hug. My parents had always loved Danny, and I'd never begrudge them that. He'd been such a big part of our lives—our family—for so long. "I'm just going to go pay our check," she said.

"It's good to see you, too, Olivia," Danny replied, watching my mom as she walked off, leaving us together at the booth. Alone.

Alone together for the first time since those four harsh words were uttered between us, shattering the tense silence of our marital home, and the front door of our townhome had slammed shut with a damning finality.

I want a divorce.

I carefully placed my glass on the table and stared down at my hands that were now resting in my lap. *How did they even get there that fast?* I absently wondered. This moment was so incredibly surreal.

Danny sighed before taking my mother's vacated seat.

"You're not even going to talk to me?" he asked, and the pain in his voice cut right into me, leaving an open, bleeding wound behind.

I closed my eyes, blinking back the tears that threatened to flow. *I'm not ready for this*, I thought to myself.

"Or look at me? Jesus, Jessie, I thought we meant more to each other than that. At least we used to. Do you hate me that much?"

My chin jolted up, and I locked eyes with him for the first time in years. The man of my dreams, who I'd loved—*love*—with all my soul. "I don't hate you," I said, my voice barely a whisper.

He smiled. It was sad, a fraction of what I would have considered a true Danny smile, but it was still a smile. As his whiskey-colored eyes scanned my face, mine did the same to his. He still had that ever-present five o'clock shadow on his strong, straight jaw, only it was a bit scruffier now. His messy, straight-out-of-bed dark hair was longer now, too. He was tan, probably from spending so much time on the field, coaching his team. Definitely still gorgeous. My eyes connected with his again, and our gazes locked. I couldn't look away, and, as it appeared, neither could he.

"You look different," he said finally.

Under normal circumstances, I might have been offended by such a statement, but our circumstances were anything but normal. This was *Danny*. I knew he hadn't meant for it to be offensive. Besides, I did look different. Hell, the last year or so of our marriage I'd completely shut down. I hadn't cared about anything, least of all my appearance. He was probably surprised to see me with clean hair, a touch of makeup, polished nails, and pants that didn't have an elastic or drawstring waistband.

"So do you," I replied. He was still as handsome as I remembered, but he looked tired, a lot less like the carefree boy I'd fallen in love with, and the easygoing man I'd been married to. He looked...weathered.

"I'm tired," he said, punctuating the statement with a perfectly timed yawn. "When I'm not working with the team, I'm working on the house. Seems my days are never-ending."

"Your uncle's old place?" I hedged, remembering Melissa saying something about it yesterday.

His face lightened up at my words. "Talking about me, Jessie?"

"Melissa has a big mouth," I grumbled. "And don't call me that," I added as an afterthought.

The light in his eyes went out, and I instantly felt bad. Jessie was a childhood nickname I couldn't stand. He was the only person I ever let get away with it, mostly because he'd always follow it up with naughty things. But it was instinctual to tell whomever said the nickname not to use it; I hadn't meant to upset him.

Those days had long since passed anyway, and we were both better off remembering that.

An awkward and uncomfortable silence rolled over the table—over the restaurant—and I glanced over my shoulder at my mom. She was sitting on a stool at the counter, quietly chatting with one of the waitresses. She'd obviously paid our tab and was now giving us what? Time alone to talk? I couldn't believe she would do that to me. I was sure she meant well, but after a lot of therapy, I knew I needed to build up to something like this, not dive right in.

"I should probably go," I said, looking back at Danny and sliding across the red vinyl bench seat. As I stood up, Danny did the same.

Then we were standing there, just inches from one another. I didn't know what to say...what to do...I felt like the entire diner was looking at us. They probably were. Oak River's golden couple, together again. But we weren't together. Not in the sense the townspeople were probably hoping for.

"Can I see you again?" he asked, tucking a loose strand of hair behind my ear. It was barely a touch, but it was intimate. It burned through my blood.

"I don't—"

"Please, Jess," he begged softly. Those damn tears came back, knocking at the backs of my eyes. "Please let's just get together and talk some time."

"I don't know. I have to go," I whispered, still backing away. I couldn't commit to seeing him again just yet. I still couldn't quite comprehend that he was standing in front of me. That he was here...in Oak River. Hell, if I was being perfectly honest, I couldn't quite comprehend that *I* was back in Oak River.

Before I could get too far, he stepped forward and wrapped his arms around me, pulling me into his chest...rubbing circles on my back with one hand while his other cradled the back of my head. My arms fell flat against my sides, hands in fists.

I couldn't move.

I couldn't breathe.

It felt *so good* to be in his arms again—to feel him and breathe him in—but it also hurt. It hurt so much. There were so many memories tied to his touch...to his scent...to him.

Memories I'd buried deep because the thought of all I'd lost was paralyzing.

He released me and took a step back, shaking his head. "I'm sorry. I just feel like I'm never going to see you again. I wanted to hold you at least one more time...just in case. I've always regretted that, you know?" He looked away, then back. I could barely see him through my tear-blurred eyes, but it looked like his eyes were a bit damp, too. "That day I left...I always wished I'd held you one last time."

He walked past me with a sad smile on his face, taking his scent and his warmth and his everything with him. Leaving me in tears...again.

I wasn't over Danny Thompson. Not by a long shot.

5

"Dinner's ready if you want to eat," Mom called through the closed door of my bedroom. I didn't answer her and soon heard her soft footsteps moving away. I knew I was hurting her, but I needed to have some time to myself.

I didn't say anything to her on the way home from The Diner. I was too upset that she left me alone with Danny. I just sat quietly, wiping the tears I couldn't get to stop spilling from my eyes. When we'd returned home, I retreated to my room to be alone and to meditate. Mindfulness and meditation were something that helped me when I felt myself getting lost in my emotions or anxiety.

About two months after our divorce was finalized—six months after Danny walked out—one of the senior partners at my law firm, Janet, staged an intervention. Well, it wasn't so much an intervention as it was her telling me that I'd better get my shit together or else. Not exactly the softest approach, but the fear of losing my job had caught my attention. It was all I had left, even if I didn't enjoy it all that much.

I started therapy and was diagnosed with major depressive disorder as a result of my infertility. No surprise there. I was prescribed antidepressants and saw a shrink for therapy twice a week for several months. Eventually I moved to weekly sessions, then every other week, and now I just checked in on occasion if I felt like I needed to. I'd shown marked improvement after about nine months, and eventually weaned myself off the medication, having never wanted to be on it in the first place, but I wasn't cured, and I still had triggers. Danny was obviously a big one, but I was armed with tools and techniques to get myself through difficult times.

At that moment, I was laying on my bed, practicing one of the meditation techniques I enjoyed which involved clenching and releasing my muscles from head to toe. For the most part it was working, and I was finding my happy place: a pink sand beach with clear blue water and palm trees dotting the shoreline. Long ago, I promised myself I would visit this place one day. I had escaped there in my head frequently, but I had no idea where it existed outside of my imagination.

After a few more minutes of deep breaths and some muscle tightening, I felt a little more human. I rolled off of my childhood bed and checked my appearance in the mirror, all around the edges were photographs of Melissa and I as tweens. I eyed the silver infinity keychain Danny had given me for our one-month anniversary before taking in my appearance. The puffiness under my brown eyes had dissipated some, and they were no longer bloodshot from the tears. I made a quick trip to the bathroom to wash my face, before heading down to the kitchen to have dinner with my parents.

Growing up, the six of us always ate dinner around the large, formal dining room table. Since it was just me and my folks, dinner was at the smaller kitchen table.

"Don't be too hard on your mom," Dad whispered as I walked by his seat at the table. "She feels awful about what happened this afternoon."

I squeezed his shoulder and offered a small smile. "It's all right. It wasn't a big deal." He gave me a look that said he knew I was lying but returned the smile all the same.

I sidled up to my mother who was standing at the counter moving mixed vegetables from a pot into a serving bowl and rested my head on her shoulder. "I'm sorry if I upset you," I told her.

Distancing myself from my family over the years meant they never saw me at my lowest. This afternoon's crying episode was not my lowest by far, but it rendered my loving parents speechless and at a loss as to what they could do to help me. They'd just never seen me so upset. And my mom was a fixer, so it couldn't have been easy staying downstairs while one of her children was so upset.

"No," Mom started, setting the now empty pot back down on the stovetop. "I'm sorry. I wasn't thinking about what seeing Danny after all this time would do to you. I thought you two could use a minute to talk. I didn't think it would upset you. I was wrong, sweetheart."

I lifted my head from her shoulder and shook it. "You didn't do anything wrong, Mom. I just..." *have issues,* "...wasn't prepared to see him is all. I haven't seen him since the divorce. It brought back a lot of memories."

It wasn't a lie. Seeing Danny *had* brought back a lot of memories. Some good and some bad. None of which I had been ready for. *Thinking* about him was one of my triggers. Seeing him...well, I wasn't really sure if there was a rating on the SUDS scale—subjective units of distress, according to my shrink—for that. Externally, I thought I'd handled myself pretty well. Internally, I was a puddle of mush.

But Mom didn't need to feel the guilt of that. It wasn't her fault; it was mine. I'd handled things so poorly near the end of our marriage, and in the years that followed. It was my fault our marriage crumbled, and it was my fault I shrunk into myself and never got appropriate closure. Danny had been my best friend, my high school sweetheart, my boyfriend, my lover, and my husband. There was never any animosity between us. Not one time. Not even at the worst of times. We just loved, and then loved harder. It was my absolute indifference in the end that split us up. I'd become numb, lost in my own head.

Mom gave me a small nod, but I knew she saw right through me. She and my dad were too good at reading their kids.

I carried the vegetables and rice to the table while Mom carried a large platter of baked chicken. There were only three of us eating tonight, but she cooked for a small army. She had always done that, never knowing when one of us would unexpectedly have a friend over for dinner. We set everything down, took our seats, and began the ritual of passing each of the dishes around so everyone could get their helping. Even though we were sitting at the smaller table and everything could be accessed easily from the middle, we still passed the dishes to one another. The familiarity of the routine was comforting.

Mom and I told Dad about the condition of the house, and I told him what I'd like to do with it. He made some suggestions and assured me that Michael and his team would do a great job. He pointed out that Michael had done the renovations to their kitchen, and I looked at the room in a new light, proud of my brother. The appliances were all brand new, as were the cabinets and floors, all done in a dark stain. The new window above the sink that looked over the backyard was larger than the previous one; I'd noticed that when washing dishes with Melissa the night before. Despite the rich tones of the walls and floors, the room seemed brighter.

"That was his idea," Dad said, noticing my attention was on the window.

"Looks like it lets in a lot more light," I observed. Dad nodded as he chewed his food.

"It does," Mom said. "Michael and your dad were concerned about the dark colors in the room, but I told them I just had to have the green walls. When I saw that hunter green in the hardware store, I just loved it."

"It was the only thing she refused to budge on," Dad added.

"It's a beautiful color," I commented in between bites.

Mom smiled, truly pleased. "I'm glad you like it."

"The room looks great, really. I can't believe Michael did all this."

It wasn't that I thought my brother was incapable of doing good work, I knew he was brilliant, but I recalled many a time when he went all Godzilla on mine and Melissa's doll houses. It was nice to see that he could build and not just destroy, granted his demo years were long before he'd even hit puberty.

"He'll do a great job at your place, too," Dad assured me.

"I might even have him expand some of the windows, since they need to be replaced anyway."

After seeing Michael's work on my parents' kitchen, I was confident my father was right and that Michael would do a fantastic job. He would make my cottage something beautiful, a place where I would feel at home. It'd been a long time since I had a place like that, and I was looking forward to the fresh start.

6

The sound of tires crunching on the gravel driveway signaled the arrival of my brother. I was both excited and nervous. Excited because this was the first step in getting my house ready for the movers, and I got to spend some—hopefully—quality time with my brother in the process, and nervous because I wasn't sure we'd ever have the easy comradery we'd once shared as kids. Something was off.

I crossed the dirty living room carpet and stepped out the open front door onto the small, creaky porch. A board wobbled under my feet, and I added another thing to my mental fix-it list.

The large, white pickup truck parked next to my Audi was a beast. It could have eaten my little convertible for breakfast. On the side of the beast was a decal that said "P.T. Construction." Interesting, I thought. The P obviously stood for Price, but the T? It didn't take too long for me to figure it out. I waved as Michael got out of the driver's side of the truck and froze when Dean Thompson got out of the passenger side with a clipboard in his hand.

T for Thompson. Dean Thompson, apparently. The middle son—Danny's younger brother and a spitting image of him, at that. The same laughing eyes, messy hair, and five o'clock shadow. They could have been twins, except they were four years apart in age. *Good genes in that family*, I thought as my heart did a double beat. Three years of no Thompsons, and suddenly they were everywhere.

"Jessie!" Dean called out, jogging across the yard and hopping up the two small steps to where I was standing. Before I could get a word out in greeting, or tell him not to call me Jessie, Dean wrapped his arms around me in an unexpected embrace and spun me around.

To say I was stunned was an understatement. Shouldn't he hate me? Or at least dislike me some? His brother and I were divorced. Wasn't that a big deal? Wasn't there a bro code for that kind of thing?

He released me and took a step back, his hands resting on my upper arms as he took in my appearance. "You're a sight for sore eyes. How are you, Jess?"

"I-I'm fine," I stuttered out. Then I remembered my manners. "How are you, Dean? You look good."

He grinned that mischievous grin the brothers shared. The one that had always melted my heart. I felt a little twitch inside my chest and knew it still had that effect, only it wasn't the right Thompson brother.

"I'm good, Jess. Real good. When Mikey said he was coming to check out your place this morning, I had to tag along. It's been ages."

It had been ages. The last time I'd seen Dean I was still married to Danny. It was during one of our trips back home for the holidays...before things went bad. Deciding against a trip down memory lane, I redirected the conversation to the guys.

"I didn't realize you guys were partners," I said, nodding to the truck, then looking at Michael.

"Yeah, we started up about two years ago, after we remodeled your mom and dad's kitchen and realized we had something," Dean answered. "There's only one other construction company in town, so we figured we had a decent shot. Myers Construction does mostly residential, so we figured we'd focus on commercial."

"You sure this won't be too much?" I asked, gesturing to my house. "Sounded like you guys were pretty busy when we spoke yesterday," I said to Michael, hoping he might actually answer me. He hadn't spoken since he got out of the truck.

"Nah, you're family. We always have time for family." It was Dean who answered. Michael continued to stay silent, just staring past me at the house. This was awkward. Shouldn't it be awkward with my ex-brother-in-law, not my actual brother?

"Well, I appreciate it," I told them. "How about I show you around?" I asked, feeling a little silly for saying it since they could probably see the entire place through the open front door.

"Sounds good," Dean said, looking between Michael and me and taking the lead once again as it was clear my brother wasn't going to. "Why don't you tell us what you'd like done, then we can do a sweep and see if there's anything else."

"All right, follow me." I stepped over the threshold and walked them around the small space.

I pointed out the carpet and the walls, and told them I'd picked out paint colors and that I wanted to do the painting myself. They walked around the room, knocking on walls and checking out the windows. They opened and closed cabinets and doors, then played with the light switches and faucets. I stood off to the side, out of their way, letting them do their thing.

We reconvened on the porch after Michael and Dean did their assessment. "This might need some work, too," I said, toeing a loose board.

Michael leaned a hip against the railing, causing a few chips of old white paint to break free, while Dean squatted down to look at it. "You're probably right. I don't think it'll need a full replacement. Maybe just a few boards." He stood back up and looked between me and my brother again—my brother who hadn't said two words to me since arriving. Before Dean could speak, his cell phone chimed with an incoming message. He took it off its belt clip and tapped the screen, reading whatever came through.

I chanced a look at Michael, but he was staring off into the yard. His silent treatment was starting to piss me off. If he didn't want to take the job, he should have turned me down when I called yesterday and given me the number to the company that did the residential work. What was the point of him coming if he wasn't going to speak to me? What would he have done if Dean hadn't come with him? Would he have spoken to me then? At least I would have known where I stood had he had just blown me off from the get go. Instead he was sending me mixed signals.

I was about to give him a piece of my mind when Dean spoke up. "Sorry, I gotta run," he said, taking off down the steps. Michael made to follow him but Dean waved him off. "I'm gonna take the truck, gotta check on a delivery issue. You should stay and go over the repairs with Jess," he told Michael. I could see my brother's body stiffen at Dean's words, and it pissed me off even more. "You can give him a ride to the site when you're finished, right, Jess? It's just down the road."

I gave Dean a reluctant nod, and he grinned...and I think he...wait, did he wink at me? That little shit. He was setting us up! Delivery issue my ass. The sneaky bastard. Michael and I watched Dean get into the beast of a truck. He waved, still grinning, as he backed out of the driveway.

Michael sighed. "Let's get this over with," he said, and stomped back up the porch steps and into the house.

- 7 -

Oh, hell no. He was *not* going to act like a juvenile and get away with it. I turned to stomp into the house behind Michael, but the moment my right foot pounded down on the porch, it went straight through a rotted-out board, and I fell on my ass.

"Son of a bitch!" I yelled, yanking my foot up through the hole. I tore a hole in my leggings and lost my shoe in the process. Rubbing my hands over my face, I wondered, *could this morning get any better?*

"What's the matter?" Michael asked, poking his head out the door. "Are you okay?" he asked when he saw me on the floor.

"I'm great. My porch tried to eat my leg, and you're being a dick. Just peachy."

He looked down at my shoeless foot and the new hole in the porch and shook his head. He walked around me, down the steps, and got down on his hands and knees in the grass to look under the porch. I heard scratching noises below me for a minute before he got back on his feet and handed me my lost shoe over the railing.

"Thanks," I mumbled, shaking the dirt out of my flat before slipping it back on my foot.

He grunted a response and walked back up the steps, past me, and into the house. "You coming?" he hollered over his shoulder.

I leaned my head back and looked up at the cracked porch light. Yet another item to add to the list. Taking a couple of deep, cleansing breaths, I got up and followed him into the house. He was standing at the kitchen counter, looking over the clipboard Dean had left behind and making some notes. I walked right up to him, about to ask him if we could just hash out whatever was between us and get it out of the way, when he started speaking.

"It looks like you'll need some repairs to the front porch deck, new exterior light fixtures, and some patchwork on the walls. A couple doors aren't set right, and I'd recommend just going ahead and replacing all of them so they'll match. I don't think they make the style you have anymore so we wouldn't be able to match just one. There's only three of them and there wouldn't be much of a difference in cost. We can smooth out the popcorn ceiling, if you don't like the look, repairing the water marks while we're at it with some new drywall. Then there's the flooring and the paint. You'll want new carpeting, for sure, or hardwood. The kitchen and bathroom cabinets are outdated, but they can be refinished to look good as new, and the appliances aren't too old, so I think you'll be all right with what's here if you're not eager to replace them. I'd recommend installing ceiling fans so you don't have to run your A/C in the spring. Oh, and the windows that aren't broken aren't sealed properly. We can seal them, but they're pretty poor quality. They're single-pane so you'll end up with drafts in the winter, so you may want to replace all of them. The exterior looks pretty good. Brick stands up to weather and wear. I know a roofer who can take a good look at the roof to see the source of the leaks, but tin roofs tend to keep well, so I'd bet it's fine. Probably just condensation from the HVAC unit, so we'll have someone take a look at that. Mr. Smith had a tenant not too long ago, so my guess is the plumbing and electrical will be fine when they're turned on, but we can have people look at that, too, if you want." Michael finally looked up from the clipboard. I just stared at him. "What?" He said.

"What?" *Is he serious?*

"Yeah, what? Why are you looking at me like that?"

"You haven't said two words to me since you got here, and when you do, it's all mechanical drivel about the house. How about, 'Hey, sis, how's it going?' or 'It'll be nice working with you on this,' or even just a big fat 'Fuck you?' Why the cold shoulder, Mikey? If you didn't want to do the job, if you don't want to be around me, why didn't you just refer me to someone else? Why go through all this?" I asked, waving my hands around. I tried keeping the emotion out of my voice, but I cracked over the last few words.

"All right, Jess," he said, standing up straight and facing me with a sneer. "Fuck you."

I gasped as he pushed past me and walked out the front door. Tears filled my eyes, but I didn't let them fall. I couldn't. I had no right. My brother was clearly more upset with me than I'd realized. I was naïve to think that just because everyone else had welcomed me back with open arms that Michael would, too. He had every right to be upset with me. We didn't really hang out a lot growing up, but he'd always been the most sensitive out of all of us. Bryan, Melissa, and I were the outgoing ones, participating in all the school activities and hanging out with our friends. Michael kept to himself. He was the quiet, shy one our parents never had to worry about since he was pretty much always at home studying.

But thinking back, we'd always talked...Michael and me. In high school, when I was still living at home, I'd always checked in with him, making sure everything was okay and no one was picking on my nerdy little brother. That continued through college. When I'd make my weekly phone calls back home, I always asked to speak with him, and we'd spend some time talking about his days and his classes. I carved out time for him when I came home on breaks, too. It was a given that I'd spend time with Melissa and Bryan because we ran in the same crowds, but I didn't have that guarantee with Michael so I made sure I spent time with him. When Danny and I got married and I started my career, I still made time to talk to Mikey.

Then my world started to fall apart and I stopped. I went from talking to him at least once a week, to not speaking to him at all for nearly five years. How could I have forgotten that?

I was a terrible sister.

In my sessions with my therapist, we'd spoken about my family briefly, basically highlighting how they had always been supportive, and how I'd assumed they would always be supportive. The crux of my issues laid with Danny and my infertility, so the doctor and I hadn't really touched on my other interpersonal relationships or lack thereof. Maybe if we had, I would have thought about the dissolution of my relationship with Michael sooner.

I sighed, looking down at the clipboard he'd left on the counter. I picked it up and did a quick walk-through of the house, making sure the lights were turned off and the windows were closed. I was certain Michael would be long gone. Living in a small town meant you could pretty much walk anywhere you needed to go if you really wanted to, and I was centrally located right off Main Street, so I imagined he'd begun hoofing it to wherever his job site was.

I stepped out the front door, locking it behind me, and reached into my bag for my cell phone. I would call my mother and ask where Michael's office was, then drop off the clipboard. I wasn't about to call him. He probably wasn't ready to deal with me yet, and I couldn't blame him. I wouldn't be ready to deal with me if I were him, either.

I was looking down at my phone as I walked, so I didn't see the figure leaning up against my car until I almost bumped right into it.

I jumped, dropping my keys to the driveway.

"You scared the crap out of me!" I scolded, holding my hand flat against my chest.

"Sorry, Jessie."

- 8 -

Okay, so I lied. There were *two* people I let get away with calling me Jessie. One was Danny; the other was my little brother Michael.

"I thought you left," I said stupidly. Obviously he hadn't left since he was standing right in front of me.

He shook his head. "I'm sorry for what I said to you in there. It was out of line. *I* was out of line," he said.

"I deserved it."

"No, you didn't," he shook his head, sighing with the weight of whatever was on his mind. "That was several years of pent up frustration."

I set the clipboard and my purse on the hood of my car and leaned my butt against the door beside him, mimicking his stance. "Want to talk about it?"

He let out a deep breath and, surprising me, started talking. "In the beginning, I understood. Somewhat, I guess. I knew you were going through something, but I wasn't sure what. Mom and Dad didn't get into details. I was pretty busy with finals and getting ready to graduate, so I didn't think much about it. Then the weeks turned into months..."

"I'm so sorry, Mikey," I said, resting my hand on his crossed forearm. He shrugged as if it didn't matter, but I knew better. My silence had hurt him badly.

"A whole year went by, Jess. *A year*," he said firmly, and I flinched. "We'd never gone that long without speaking and the only saving grace, which wasn't much of one at all, was that you weren't talking to anyone else either, so at least I didn't take it personally, but I still didn't understand. I was still pissed you stopped talking to me."

"I didn't know what to say," I told him honestly. "I was so lost, Mikey. I honestly wasn't thinking about anyone but myself and everything that was going wrong."

He nodded. "I get that. I just wish you would have leaned on us. Especially Mom. She was devastated she couldn't be there for you. You don't know how many times she packed an overnight bag, ready to drive out to the city. Dad had to talk her down."

Tears filled my eyes as my heart broke for what felt like the thousandth time. I hadn't known that. "I'm sorry I caused you all so much pain. I was so depressed, Mike. I wasn't thinking about anyone. I was barely even thinking about myself. I just wanted to...lose myself. I don't know how to explain it."

"I understand," he said simply, and the deep sadness in his eyes told me he *did* understand. It was an emptiness that only someone who had also experienced a deep grief would recognize.

Michael had gone through something while I was gone.

"What happened?" I asked him, and his sad eyes lifted to mine with surprise. "The look in your eyes tells me you know a thing or two about loss."

He nodded and looked off into the woods behind the cottage. "I had a girlfriend," he started, and my heart broke at the past tense and the sorrow in his voice. Did she leave him? Had she died? "Kara. We met at the beginning of freshman year."

Kara, I said to myself, wracking my memory. I remembered him talking about a girlfriend long ago when I'd call him, and I vaguely remembered the name Kara. So much of that time in my life was fuzzy. "You brought her home for Christmas?" I remembered him with a petite brunette at a holiday or two. They seemed happy.

"Sophomore and senior year," he nodded.

His sophomore year was the last Christmas I'd spent with my family. I'd been so fragile after the initial infertility diagnosis, then the surgery shattered what little was left holding me together. I had such little hope left at that point, even though we hadn't yet tried IVF. I hadn't even wanted to see anyone for Christmas, but Danny put his foot down. That was the beginning of his frustration with me, but it certainly wasn't the end.

"What happened?" I asked, squeezing his arm.

His eyes turned glassy, and I leaned my head on his shoulder in silent support. My little

53

brother was taller than me now, so it was the best I could do. I hated that whatever happened between him and Kara had hurt him so deeply.

"She left."

"You guys broke up?" I asked, uncertain as to what he meant.

"No. Yes. I don't know." He kicked at the gravel. "I guess so. One day everything was fine. We graduated, spent the summer together...we had plans that included each other. They always included each other." He furrowed his eyebrows as if he still didn't understand what had gone wrong. I could relate, sort of. Danny and I always had plans that included each other, only I knew what went wrong. *I* went wrong. "Then one day she was gone," he added solemnly.

"She left without saying anything?" I frowned. That didn't seem right.

He nodded. "We were living together. I bought a small house on Cedar with my inheritance." My siblings and I each got a modest inheritance from our grandparents, our mom's parents, when they'd passed away. "It wasn't much, but it was enough for us. She loved it. At least, I thought she did. She'd gone to school for photojournalism and got a spot on the paper with Dad and Melissa. It was low level, she wouldn't let me call in any favors because she wanted to earn her way, but she was proud of it and I was proud of her." He looked at me with tears in his eyes. "We were happy, Jess. We weren't living the American Dream just yet, but we were getting there. I was going to propose to her on our four-year

54

anniversary. Then one day I went home, and she was gone. All her things, every trace of her...just gone."

"Have you heard from her since?" I couldn't help but ask.

"Not one word," he said as he looked away from me and tried to discretely wipe his eyes. "I called her parents, even showed up at their house. They said she was abroad, took some assignment from a travel magazine or something."

"Is that true?" I asked.

"No," he scoffed. "She was terrified of flying. She never would have traveled overseas. Not even by boat."

I blew out a breath. "I'm so sorry, Michael. I should have been here for you."

"Yeah," he nodded. "You should have. And you should have let us be there for you, too."

"You're right," I nodded. We stood in silence for a few minutes, lost in our own thoughts...in our own losses...before I finally broke the silence. "How about we do something tonight, just me and you?" I asked, hopeful he'd say yes.

"What do you have in mind?" he asked cautiously.

"I think having a few drinks with my baby bro might be just what Dr. Todd ordered...for both of us."

"Dr. Todd?"

"My shrink."

His eyes widened briefly at that little factoid, then he nodded. "Yeah, I think drinks sound good."

"Are you still on Cedar?" I asked softly, not wanting to upset him if he'd moved away from the home he and Kara had created.

"Yeah...I couldn't bring myself to leave."

In case she came back. He didn't have to say it, I knew. It's the same reason I stayed in the townhouse months after Danny had moved out. After we separated and eventually divorced. I think some part of me hoped he might come back and wanted him to be able to find me if he did. He never came back, though. And, apparently, neither did Kara.

"Text me your address. I'll meet you at your place and we'll walk together to The Bar." Yes...The Bar. We lived in *that* town. The Bar and The Diner. That's where it ended, though. The rest of the establishments in our small town were named after their founders or Oak River itself. "You got a couch your big sister can crash on after she drinks too much?" I asked, picking up my purse off the hood and walking around to the driver's side of my car.

Michael grabbed the clipboard before he tucked his large frame into the passenger seat. "I'll do you one better," he said as we buckled up. "I've got a guest bedroom. You can sleep on a bed."

"Sounds perfect." I said with a smile, happy the tension that was between us finally dissolved.

9

The Bar was standing room only. Since it was Friday night, and The Bar was the only location for nightlife in Oak River, it was to be expected. As planned, I'd driven to Michael's house and we walked over together. There was a *Cheers*-like atmosphere, and everyone seemed to know Mikey's name. Fortunately, no one seemed to recognize me, not yet anyway, so I was able to avoid any awkward pleasantries. The crowd seemed young—or younger than me, rather—guys Mikey's age and maybe students from the nearby university. It was probably why I wasn't approached.

Michael got us each a beer, and we found an open spot to stand in the back near the pool tables. I liked the position because it gave me an unobstructed view of the entire space—not that it was all that big. The Bar was a typical, small town, hole-in-the-wall establishment. It was maybe two thousand square feet with the bar resting along one long wall, two pool tables lining the other, a small stage for live bands and karaoke nights in the back with a tiny dance floor in front of it, and a few high-top tables scattered throughout. Everything was wooden, from the stained floors to the bar top to the paneled walls. There were a few dart boards hanging here and there, and the jukebox in the corner flashed a rainbow of colors in the otherwise brown space.

I could count on one hand the amount of times I'd been in The Bar. I turned twenty-one while in college, so most of the bars I'd gone to had been in the city. Danny and I had stopped in once or twice when we were home for the holidays to catch up with friends, but we spent most of our time with our families on our short trips to Oak River. Plus, I'd cut out alcohol when we started trying to conceive and, subsequently, bars. Now that I was back home, I'd probably spend more time at The Bar, so I'd better get used to it. Classic rock tunes blasted from the jukebox, and I found myself starting to relax, bopping my head to the beat.

"Well, look at what the cat dragged in," Michael said suddenly.

I followed his stare and startled as my eyes landed on our older brother, Bryan. Melissa was right behind him.

"Hey, sibs!" she called out, raising her hands in the air and swinging her jean-clad hips to the beat of the Bob Seger song that was playing.

"What are you guys doing here?" I asked, leaning in to give each of them a hug. I couldn't remember the last time the four of us all hung out together. It definitely wasn't in a bar, since this was my first time out drinking with Mikey.

"A birdie told me you and Mikey were having a night out on the town, so I called up Bry and we decided to crash your party."

A birdie we all fondly knew as *Mom*, undoubtedly. I looked over to Michael who didn't seem bothered at all and shrugged. "The more the merrier. I'm glad you guys came. Can I get you guys a beer? Should we do a pitcher now that there's more of us?" I wondered aloud.

"Blech," Melissa said. "I don't drink that crap. I'll go get myself a cocktail."

"Bry?" I asked.

"I'm Melissa's D.D." He shrugged with a small smile. He was leaning against the wall beside Michael with his arms crossed. His large build and don't mess with me stance, along with his black t-shirt, jeans, and black boots made him look like a bouncer or a bodyguard. It was hard to believe that guy dressed in a suit most days and worked in a stuffy office.

"Oh, you guys should just walk with us back to Mikey's and crash there. That's what I'm doing."

"Inviting people to my house, Jess?" Michael smarted off, making me roll my eyes.

"You can invite yourself over to my house whenever you want," I offered in return.

Michael bent forward, laughing so hard he snorted. "Right. That place should be condemned."

I frowned. "That wasn't very nice. That place is going to be my home."

"I know, I'm just picking on you. You're such an easy target. I'll help make your house a home."

His words warmed my heart. There was no greater feeling in the world than being part of my family again. I couldn't help but think how my emotional journey could have been so much different had I stayed in contact with my family and let them help me heal. Or if I had just let Danny in when he'd tried to break through my walls. Instead, I pushed everyone away and ended up even more alone than I'd been before.

My siblings and I chatted about everything and nothing. Bryan stayed the dutiful designated driver and didn't have so much as a drop of alcohol. Michael, Melissa, and I, on the other hand, got completely inebriated. I couldn't remember the last time I let loose and had fun. I was laughing at all the jokes—whether they were funny or not—and it had to be said, Michael's jokes were never funny.

I was just straightening myself up after being folded over in laughter from Mikey's latest, when I felt that slow buzz in my veins—and I'm not talking about the buzz of the booze, I was long past that point. This was different. A hum. An awareness. This was *him*.

In my intoxicated state, I didn't seem to care that we were divorced, that I didn't know how to speak around him anymore, or that the mere sight of him could cause me to have a nervous breakdown. I just wanted a glimpse. Just a quick glimpse at Danny, and maybe a whiff, too. He smelled so good, and I missed him so, so much.

My eyes darted wildly across the crowded bar, and like a magnet drawn to another magnet, or a great big piece of metal—or something—my eyes found his. He was watching me with that same sad smile he'd been wearing at The Diner. I hated that I put that sad smile on his sad face again. I wanted to apologize. I wanted to hug him and smell him and—

"Whoa, where do you think you're going?" Bryan asked as he pulled me back into our little circle by one of the belt loops on my jeans.

"I was just—" I trailed off when I saw the sympathetic look in Bryan's eyes. He knew what I was trying to do. I'd probably have to thank him when I was sober—if I remembered. "I screwed everything up. I made him sad. I made all you sad. All because I was sad. I'm an asshole."

Bryan pulled me into his chest just as the first sob broke free. It's a good thing he did, too, because it was loud, even muffled by his shirt. He rubbed my back and shushed me as I cried; I wrapped my arms tightly around my big brother. I was so damn emotional all of a sudden.

I'm an emotional drunk! That was something I'd never known about myself.

"She's fine...I don't think that's a good idea...thanks, we've got her..." I couldn't hear the voice of whomever Bryan was talking to, but I could only imagine that it was one person. My one person. I wanted to pick up my head and look, but there was one tiny drop of self-preservation that I hadn't cried out left in my repertoire, and it told me to stay put. So I nestled deeper into Bryan's chest and closed my eyes.

61

10

"It's a cookie!"

"No, it's a meatball."

"Pizza!"

Dad turned away from the white board and rolled his eyes at his team. I could tell by the look on his face that he wanted to yell the right answer at them, but if he spoke, he forfeited his turn. That was how we played Pictionary when the Thompson's came over for family game night.

Mr. Thompson returned to the living room with a beer in each hand, one for him and one for my dad. "American Pie," he said as he sat down, setting the bottles on coasters.

Dad spun around and pointed at Mr. T. "Yes!" He walked over to the couch and they high-fived each other.

Did I mention that we played different themes each week? That week was movies.

"All right, girls. We got this," Mrs. T said as she went up to the board for her turn. She pulled a postcard off the pile and read it. Then she grinned. Melissa, Mom, and I exchanged smiles. We were down by two points, but it was still early.

Bryan flipped the timer and yelled "go," and Mrs. T began drawing.

First she drew a tall rectangle with a...a phone. It was a phone booth! "Phone booth!" I shouted. She turned and pointed at me, but kept drawing. A stick figure...a cape...

"Superman!" Melissa called out.

"Yes!" Mrs. T yelled, high-fiving all of us as she returned to her seat.

The guys all rolled their eyes. They had the worst sportsmanship on game night.

"Dan, you're up," Dad said.

Danny stood from his place on a beanbag seat on the floor and walked over to the cards, pulling one off the top. His shoulders slumped as he read the movie title and I knew it had to be one of the ones me and Melissa put in the pile. We always added movies that would be difficult to draw, especially if you didn't know what it was about.

Melissa reached over and flipped the timer on the table, and Danny began to draw. He made a circle that sort of looked like a hamburger on its side, then added a line that looked like a string. Was it a yo-yo? I had no idea where he was going with that, then Melissa leaned over and whispered in my ear. "Ya-Ya."

Laughter erupted from my chest and Danny glared at me. I immediately quieted down. He was trying to draw Divine Secrets of the Ya-Ya Sisterhood. It was a new movie in theaters, and when Melissa and I had seen the title, we knew we had to add it to game night.

The guys' team guessed that it was a yo-yo, but they couldn't figure the rest out before time ran out. We high-fived, and Danny glared as he returned to his seat.

It was my turn. I got up and picked a card from the middle of the deck. There was no rule on where we had to pick from, so I always picked from the middle.

I recognized Danny's handwriting immediately. The movie was Coyote Ugly. I wanted to guess that he'd chosen that title because the girls all sucked at drawing animals, but little did he know, I could put a stick figure on a bartop and Melissa would get it right away. I smirked at him and he frowned. Game on.

Mikey flipped the timer and I got started. My bar was nothing more than a rectangular box with some stools in front of it. I drew some shelves behind the bar with bottles of alcohol on them. Then came the stick figure in a short skirt.

"Cocktail," Mom yelled. Close, but not quite. Come on, Melissa.

"Road House." I wasn't even sure what Mrs. T was talking about.

"Oh!" Thatta girl, Mel. "Coyote Ugly!"

"Whoohoo!" I did a little dance on my way back to the couch. I was starting my second year of cheerleading, so I had a few moves. I caught Danny watching me shake my hips, and he wasn't glaring. Hmm.

"All right, we need a tiebreaker." Mom announced. When we had tiebreakers, each team drew the same thing and whichever team got it first won. If they guessed at the same time, or it was too close to determine, we did it again and again until we had a clear winner. We were a pretty competitive bunch.

Mom went against Mr. T in the first, and hopefully only, tiebreaker round. I had a good feeling about this.

They each looked at the card, then we counted to three as a group, and they began drawing. There was no timer during tiebreakers.

Mom drew a wavy line across her side of the board, then a boat. So it was a movie with a boat.

"Jaws?" I called out.

Mom shook her head, and kept drawing. There was now a person in the water beside the boat.

"Titanic?" One of the guys shouted. I looked at Mr. T's drawing. It was similar to Mom's.

Mom erased the boat and re-drew it under the water line. So it was a sunken ship, but it wasn't Titanic. What other movies had a shipwreck? Mom drew something that looked like a tornado...but Twister didn't make sense. Or Wizard of Oz. Could it be a storm? A storm that capsized the boat? Oh!

"The Perfect Storm!"

Mr. T groaned as Mom jumped up and down, clapping her hands.

"Girls rule, boys drool," Melissa said to the other team, sticking out her tongue. Mom, Mrs. T, and I followed suit, sticking out tongues out at the guys.

When we were finished celebrating, we lined up and shook hands with the other team. It was kind of silly, but it was our parents' way of making sure we all left game night on good terms. No grudges.

Danny and I were last in line, and when it was our turn, my breath caught as he leaned forward to whisper in my ear. "You did good, Jessie." I shivered as his warm breath moved the loose tendrils of hair around my ear. Danny pulled back and grinned at me. He had the cutest smile. It was always a little crooked on the right side, like he was up to something.

And maybe he was.

He'd asked me out three days later.

"Does Michael have a cat?" I groaned, wishing I was back inside my dream of one of our fun family game nights, rather than lying in a strange bed with a horrible hangover.

"What? No. Why?" Melissa groaned back.

"Because I think his cat threw up in my mouth."

"He doesn't have a cat."

"Was it you?"

"You're so disgusting!" Melissa whined, hitting me in the head with her pillow. "No one threw up in your mouth, except maybe you."

"Not so loud," I whisper-hissed. My head was throbbing. My skull ached where the soft pillow had hit it, and I actually felt my pulse in my brain. *Throb. Throb. Throb.* I refused to open my eyes, instead keeping them clenched shut, so I had no idea what time it was.

"Maybe next time you won't drink all the shots in the bar," she said. Her smug tone irritated the crap out of me. If I remembered correctly, she was right by my side, feeding me those shots after...after I saw Danny and completely broke down. Like a fool.

"Why are you here, anyway?" I asked, bitterness coating the words. If she wasn't going to join my pity party, she could leave.

"You begged me to stay last night. You begged Bryan to stay, too. It was kind of adorable how excited you were over the prospect of a sibling slumber party."

A small smile graced my lips. I didn't remember that part of the evening. "And you stayed."

"We all did. Well, Bry might be gone by now, but he was making his bed on the couch when Mike and I finally wrangled you in here."

I rolled over towards my sister, not letting my nausea from the movement deter me. When I bumped into her side, I blindly wrapped my arm around her. "Thanks for being here."

"Thanks for letting me be here," she said, patting my arm. "But damn, your breath really does smell like vomit. Can you go brush your teeth?"

I opened my eyes and glared at her, then blew out a quick breath right in her face and rolled quickly in the other direction. As suspected, I got hit in the back with another pillow as I sat up. At least it wasn't my head this time. I was lightheaded when I stood up—still a little drunk, apparently—and I'm not talking about that little hangover buzz you sometimes have after a night of drinking, I'm talking *drunk*. How much alcohol did I consume last night?

I balanced on the furniture and the walls to get myself to the bathroom, where I promptly relieved myself, washed my hands and my face, and brushed my teeth. I was thankful someone had the foresight to bring my toiletry bag into the bathroom. Maybe it was me. No, that was doubtful since it would have required some sense and I didn't seem to have any of that left.

On the way back to the bedroom, the smell of coffee resulted in me taking a sharp right turn down the hall towards the kitchen. Coffee had the potential to cure just about anything. Slowly making my way down the hall—hands on the wall still to keep from falling—I found Bryan sitting at Michael's small kitchen table with the morning paper.

"Good morning, Sunshine," he greeted, looking up at me with a smile. A smile that quickly turned into a frown. "You look rough. I knew I should have stopped you before the tequila."

"Tequila?" That explained it. I did not do tequila well.

"Yep. Mike and Mel might as well have just bought the bottle. Or bottles."

I cringed, then groaned as I slipped into the seat beside him. "That's why I woke up with a hairball in my mouth," I muttered to myself.

"What?" Bryan asked, raising his eyebrow.

"Nothing," I said, trying to shake my head. The movement made my brain rattle and I stopped just as soon as I'd started. "I need coffee." I moved to get up, but Bryan put his hand on my arm.

"I'll get it," he said.

I smiled at him in thanks and watched as he stood and made his way around the kitchen, first grabbing a mug and filling it with the hot goodness, then opening another cabinet and grabbing a bottle of ibuprofen. A tinge of sadness rolled through me as I watched my older brother move through my little brother's kitchen with such familiarity. I should have known Michael's kitchen that well, too.

I made a tiny, ridiculous little goal to know my way around my siblings' homes. At least around their kitchens, I didn't want to come off as a complete psycho rummaging through their closets and stuff. I just wanted to know them in that small, insignificant (yet so significant) way they all seemed to know each other. The fact that I was so unfamiliar with their lives now was no one's fault but my own, but it was something I planned to fix.

Bryan set the mug and a couple pills down in front of me and gestured to the sugar and creamer. "Thank you. I drink my coffee black, though."

"Me, too," he said, and I smiled, pleased we had that in common, and even more pleased that I now knew how one of my siblings took their coffee. One down, two to go.

***

"And he was just sitting there, stunned, covered in mud and river water. He had no idea what the hell happened."

I clutched my stomach as I laughed at Bryan's story. He just finished telling me about when he and Michael went on a fishing trip for a mutual friend's bachelor party. Apparently Michael and the boat trailer didn't get along, and Michael ended up on his ass in the muddy bank of the river.

"How are you even alive?" Melissa grunted at me as she walked into the kitchen. "I thought for sure I'd find you passed out in the bathroom."

"I smelled coffee," I shrugged, holding up my cup. She nodded, as if that made all the sense in the world. It did, of course.

"Y'all do realize it's not even eight yet," Michael said as he joined us a moment later, scratching his head and squinting his eyes at the small digital clock numbers on the microwave. "We went to bed like four hours ago."

"Someone's grouchy in the morning," Melissa taunted him in a goofy voice pausing in the preparation of her coffee to ruffle his hair. Cream and two sugars. I wasn't surprised.

Michael twisted away, glaring at her. "Someone is not used to having a houseful of people making a ruckus at seven forty-five in the morning."

"Sorry, Mikey," I said in the sweetest voice I could muster given my state. I still sounded like an eighty-year-old smoker. "Did I sing last night? Or scream?" I wondered out loud.

"No, but you were talking so loud, it was like you swallowed a megaphone," Michael said.

"Huh." That was an interesting visual. I picked up a spoon off the table and looked at my reflection as I opened my mouth as wide as I could. I didn't even think my fist could fit in there, let alone a megaphone. The side of Melissa's lip lifted in disgust as she watched me attempt to put my hand in my mouth. I shrugged, I honestly didn't know what the hell I was doing either. Blame it on the alcohol.

"Why is it chicks get louder the more they drink?" Michael asked Bryan, who shrugged his shoulders in response.

"Hey," Melissa scolded. "We're your sisters. Don't refer to us as *chicks*. Show some respect."

Michael rolled his eyes as he lifted up the now empty coffee pot. "Really?"

"I'll brew another batch," I told him, feeling guilty for completely taking over his house. If it hadn't been for me, he'd be sleeping in with the place to himself.

"Don't worry about it, I got it." I took note of the cabinet where he retrieved the filters and the coffee grounds and stored it in my memory bank, right next to the location of the cabinet with the pain pills. Never knew when I might be hungover at Michael's house again. Hopefully not for a very, very long time.

"So what's on the agenda for today?" Melissa asked, directing the question at no one in particular.

"The kids have a soccer game at ten, so I'll need to head out soon."

"Can I come?" I asked immediately. I wanted to make up for all the lost time, and if that meant cheering at sporting events, volunteering for bake sales, and camping with the kids' scout groups, I would do just that. *Aunt of the Year* right here, ladies and gentlemen. It was happening. I just wouldn't say it aloud because then Melissa would fight me for the title. I'd rather her not know there was a competition.

When Bryan turned to me with a smile on his face, I knew I'd said the right thing. "Of course. We'd love to have you. They play at the rec fields."

I grinned, excited to be making plans with my brother and his kids for the day. I couldn't wait to really, truly be Auntie Jessica to Emma, Luke, and Evan.

"Why don't we all go?" Melissa suggested.

"Sounds good to me," Michael added. He sat down at the table with his coffee—sugar only—and swiped the paper from Bryan.

We continued to chat about random things, and I found myself making plans for different events and activities with my brothers and sister. It warmed me from head to toe. It had been so long since I had that. Long before I stopped talking to my family even. That distance happened when I moved away to go to college and didn't come home for more than a quick visit here and there. I was just so busy, always so busy. It was nice to slow down for a minute—or ten.

Being able to get a pedicure with Melissa, hit the flea market just outside of town with Michael, or sit on the sidelines of a soccer game with Bryan were things I'd never take for granted again.

11

"I take it the four of you had fun last night?" Mom asked, glancing over at me, Melissa, and Michael.

Sitting on the bleachers alongside field three of the rec fields—a large recreational sports complex at the edge of town between Oak River and the university—we were a sight to see, all decked out in sunglasses and comfy clothes. Melissa and I were in yoga pants and sweatshirts to ward off the morning chill, and Michael was in jeans and a long sleeve t-shirt. Bryan was down on the field next to Karla with Emma and Evan. He looked perfectly fine, though; probably because he drank nothing last night. I supposed that having three kids aged three to seven meant you didn't have time to be hungover. To be perfectly honest, I envied him that, but in a good way. My brother had a wonderful family and I loved every bit of the happiness reflected on his face.

Maybe someday I'd get to experience that same kind of joy.

"So much fun," Melissa said, trying to sound chipper, but falling flat.

"If you were home I could have fixed you a Bloody Mary for breakfast. Nothing cures a hangover like a little hair of the dog that bit ya."

The three of us turned our heads to gape at her. "Mom," I teased with a smile.

She shrugged her shoulders, hiding her grin. "I was young once, too." We shook our heads and returned our eyes to the field. It didn't matter how old we were or how human we knew our parents to be, learning certain things about them—like the fact that they had a hangover cure—was still weird.

***

Have you ever watched five-year olds play soccer? Chaos, plain and simple. There were eleven players from each team on the field at a time, so over twenty kids at once. All of them were charging for the ball at the same time, kicking their little legs like tiny Rockettes in shin guards. The goalie didn't stay in the goal, either. Oh no, he or she ran after the ball like the rest of them, not wanting to be left out. You couldn't see the ball from the bleachers, but you knew where it was because of the cluster of twenty-two kids that moved around the field like a herd of small cattle. They scored on their own nets and played the ball right off the field— sometimes onto other fields—all the while being as adorable as ever in their little uniforms and pads. I couldn't be more proud of Luke. I was, however, interested in seeing if the seven-year olds were any better; Emma's game was next.

I was about to get up and get another coffee from the concession stand when activity on one of the larger fields beyond the soccer game caught my attention. It wasn't children's soccer being played on that field, but larger humans in way more padding. They were playing...football, or at least preparing to play. And I would have recognized the green and gold team colors on the practice jerseys any day. Those were Oak River High School players, which meant...

My eyes sought him out before my brain could command it not to. Danny was standing on the sidelines in black track pants and a white t-shirt with a green and gold Oak River ball cap on his head and a whistle around his neck. He looked like a coach. A sudden and overwhelming sense of pride filled my chest for him. It was his dream come true. *He was doing it.* And he was doing it at a school he loved.

I decided to skip the second coffee—for now—and stare at him unabashedly. I couldn't see the expressions on his face, but I could almost picture them from his body language. I knew him well enough to pick up on certain cues, like when he ran one hand through his hair, he was frustrated. If he ran both hands through his hair, all bets were off and you'd better just get the hell out of his way. He did that a lot at the end of our marriage...I made him do that a lot was more like it.

He was doing a lot of the single hand hair swipes as he paced the side of the field. I loved seeing him in his element...seeing him so complete. Growing up, he knew he hadn't wanted to play football professionally. He played well enough in high school and got a scholarship to college, where he played all four years. He'd always planned to coach though. Coach and teach. He received his bachelor's degree in education, and even continued on for a master's degree in physical education at night while I was in law school. We didn't see a lot of each other those days, but things were still mostly good. Coaching football was always Danny's goal though. And he'd achieved it. I never got to see him coach. He taught high school English when we were married; he hadn't landed a coaching job when we were still together. Deep down, I think he was holding out for *this* opportunity. At our old high school. I was so happy for him, and I wished things weren't so...damaged, so I could celebrate that accomplishment with him.

But I lost that right when I lost my husband...when I let him go.

***

I spent most of Emma's game, which luckily for my lazy butt and wandering eyes was on the same field as Luke's, watching Danny and the football team practice. It brought back memories of when Danny played and I was a cheerleader. Our practices would run simultaneously, so the drills I witnessed were vaguely familiar. It didn't surprise me that Danny had his boys using some of the same playbook he had, especially considering his team had made it to the state championship our junior and senior years.

When the game ended, I said goodbye to my family, deciding to walk home. I told them I needed the fresh air, which was the absolute truth. I did need fresh air, only it wasn't due to the hangover as they'd assumed. It was because of Danny.

Seeing him after so long, three days in a row, in an element that was so familiar, made me feel things I hadn't felt in a long time. It wasn't just the sadness, it was the good things, too. I remembered the wonderful times we'd shared. There were so many to choose from. Moments where Danny made me feel like I was the most special girl in the world. He tried to make me feel that way straight through the end, but my body's refusal to do what it was meant to do killed any positive image I'd ever held of myself. I couldn't possibly be special if I was damaged...worse than that...if I was broken. Danny never implied that, though. It was my own twisted cognitions. I realized that now, and I probably knew it then, too, but there was no going back.

One end of Main Street to the other was about four miles, stretching the length of Oak River. I only had about a mile of the road to walk before I'd make the turn onto the side road that would take me back to my parents' house. As I approached that side road, I decided to go straight and head to the park about another half mile down. It was a small children's park, mostly abandoned for the larger and more colorful plastic playground structures at the elementary school, but it held a lot of fond memories of me and Danny.

The soft sound of my footsteps on the old wood chips echoed between the trees. It was so quiet, I could hear my heartbeat if I listened close enough. I paused at the edge of the park and looked around. The paint had faded over time and the jungle gym was no longer the vibrant colors of my teen years. The wood was nearly black from years of wear and tear. Some spots were rotted. Paint had chipped off the metal monkey bars and scattered ladders. I absently wondered why no one had ever torn it down, surely it was a hazard. Nevertheless, I was grateful it was still there. The old, metal swing set looked sturdy enough, and that's where I was headed.

I sat on the cold, rusted metal seat and kicked off, gathering my rhythm pretty quickly, and bending and swaying accordingly. I leaned my head back and looked up at the sky, picturing moments in the past, just like this one. Only in my memories, Danny was behind me, his hands caressing my waist or shoulders on each backwards swing. He was always sneaking in a touch, innocent and...less than innocent.

Oh, how I missed his touch. I'd stopped letting him touch me at the end of our relationship, even going to far as to flinch away from him. How I must have hurt him...

The sky and the trees became blurry, and it was only then that I realized I was crying. I stopped pumping my legs and the swing slowed. Damn those memories. Damn me for screwing everything up. Damn me for being broken and—

Something touched my back as the swing stilled near the bottom…a hand.

And not just any hand…*his* hand.

- 12 -

I laughed giddily as he pushed me on the swing, my legs straight out in front of me.

Instead of partying at the lake with our friends to celebrate the end of our final year of high school, we were at the old park. It was one of our most favorite places, since it was mostly abandoned. Just me and Danny against the world.

"We're getting ready to start chapter two," Danny said as I swung. "You ready?"

"I'm ready for anything with you," I told him truthfully.

I was a little apprehensive about the future, about finally leaving our small town and heading off into the real world—or at least to a college campus—but I was ready for it anyway. It didn't matter what life threw at us, as long as we were together.

He took hold of the chains as I swung back and slowed the swing. I leaned back to look up at him. His piercing brown eyes gazed at me adoringly, and I smiled back. I loved him so much.

"I love you, Jessica Lynn Price."

"I love you, Daniel Andrew Thompson."

He leaned forward and took me in an upside-down kiss. It was a weird sensation, a backwards feeling, but just as amazing and tingle-inducing as every other kiss we'd shared. When we broke apart, he rested his forehead against mine for a moment.

"I'm going to marry you one day," he whispered, before righting himself and giving me another push.

My answering grin was brighter than the sun as the warm spring air brushed my flushed cheeks.

"Shh," he said as I let out a sob. His presence and the memory...it was too much. He stepped around the front of the swing and wrapped me in his arms. "Just let it out, Jessie," he urged me.

I did. I cried more tears on that swing than I did during the last year and a half of our marriage. I let down all my walls, all my barriers...I let it all spill out on Danny.

Pressed against his warm chest, I felt the hard ridges of muscle under his t-shirt. They were familiar—he was familiar—and safe. I felt so incredibly safe in his arms...safe and loved. After all these years, I still felt it. His body still emanated that same heat towards me that it had when we were teenagers in love.

I stiffened at that thought. *Love.* We weren't in love anymore. Our love story had ended. Danny must have felt the shift in my body because he let me go and stepped back.

"I'm sorry," I mumbled, turning away from him and wiping the wetness from my cheeks.

"You don't ever have to be sorry with me, Jess."

"Don't I, though?" I asked, glancing at him over my shoulder. I pushed him away at a time when we'd both been grieving, essentially. Maybe we hadn't lost a child, exactly, but we'd lost hope...and opportunity and normalcy.

He took a step towards me. "Never," he said with such finality that I couldn't argue.

He'd been like that in the end...firm and confident in his love for me. He truly believed we could weather whatever storm was sent our way. On this playground years ago, I'd believed that, too. I wish I'd remained that confident. I wish I'd trusted in him. I wish I hadn't been so stuck in my own head—my own misery—that I could have let him in.

Maybe things would have ended up differently.

Maybe...

"I didn't know you were planning to come back to Oak River," he said after a few quiet moments.

Honestly, how would he have known? It's not like we'd spoken recently, or at all. Our divorce was handled through lawyers. I went through my lawyer anyway, I didn't know if Danny was an active participant. I was not present, mentally or physically.

"Me neither," I admitted, crossing my arms over my chest and running my hands up and down my arms. I wasn't cold, but I felt as though I needed to hold myself together. "It just sort of happened...the opportunity to buy Mr. Smith's practice."

"Yeah...same here. Coach Murray called me and told me he was retiring."

Maybe it was fate intervening. Maybe the world was giving us a second chance.

I had worked part-time filing at Mr. Smith's office throughout high school, it was where my interest in law was born. I loved the idea of law and order. And Danny had always idolized his high school football coach. He aspired to be just like him. And there we both were...following directly in our mentors' footsteps.

"It's funny how things work out," Danny added, seeming to follow my train of thought.

Was it? Was it funny that we ended up back in Oak River at the same time? Was it a coincidence? Or was it more than that?

"Look," Danny continued, "I don't want to upset you. I'll keep my distance from you, Jessie. If that's what you want. It's just so damn hard." He looked up at the overcast sky. "I swear...when you're around, I can feel it. I was driving by here and something told me to stop. It's like I'm drawn to you—only to you— and you pull me right in. I still love you as much today as I did ten years ago."

I gasped, closing my damp eyes, surprised there were any tears left to leak out. *He still loved me.*

Why did you leave? I wanted to ask him that, but it wasn't fair. He hadn't wanted to leave. I'd forced his hand. I practically pushed him out the door.

"I'm sorry...I said I didn't want to upset you, but I did anyway." He sounded regretful, and I bet if I turned around, I'd see the same shadows in his eyes I'd seen there three years ago. I just couldn't face him, though.

I felt him approach me, the heat of his chest mere inches from my back, and my body came alive yet again.

"I'm here, Jessie. Whenever you're ready...I'm here." I felt a quick whisper of a touch on the back of my head, in my hair. *Was it his lips?*

I listened to his footsteps as he walked away, fading until there was silence in the park, save for the occasional bird chirping. I stood there, staring into the nothingness of the surrounding woods, thinking about when it all began to fall apart.

"I have good news and bad news," Dr. Rowland said as he took a seat across the antique desk. His pale, paper thin skin stretched lazily across his face; I could have sworn he was older than time. But he was the most experienced reproductive endocrinologist around, and we wanted the best.

"Good news first," Danny said from the antique patterned wingback chair beside me, squeezing my hand in a gesture of solidarity. I looked over at my husband of three years and took in his hopeful, yet terrified expression. It probably mirrored my own.

We'd come to this appointment with so much optimism, so much hope for our future family. You see, this wasn't supposed to happen to us. We were supposed to get married, spend some time just being us—Danny and Jessica Thompson—and then get pregnant. We'd both come from large families and wanted our own small brood. We were just supposed to ditch the condoms, and then it would happen.

But it didn't happen.

Not after one cycle, or two. Not after six, or twelve. Not after I'd started charting my basal body temperature, eagerly anticipating that spike that would indicate I was ovulating. I used the ovulation predictor kits, too. All signs pointed in the right direction, but nothing ever stuck. Countless dollars spent on early result pregnancy tests, just to see a single pink line in the window every damn time.

Something was wrong.

Part of me prayed the something wrong was me. I didn't want Danny to have to carry that guilt, but I knew I could. Women were built strong to deal with emotional stressors, at least that's what I believed. Danny wanted a baby so badly, and he was so sensitive. I didn't think he could handle being the problem...the cause of all the disappointment we've felt over the past year. I knew he wouldn't have wanted to let me down—to be the "cause" of our agony.

In retrospect, I should have given him more credit.

"Well, the good news is that your sperm are excellent. Your count and mobility are actually off the charts."

Danny smiled at the doctor, momentarily pleased by the compliment about his little swimmers. Then his smile turned to a frown as he quickly glanced at me. I wasn't really sure

85

what he saw when his brown eyes locked with mine, but I imagine it wasn't good.

"It's going to be all right, baby," he assured me, squeezing my hand again.

His assurance made me angry because, in that moment, how the hell did he know? The doctor hadn't even gotten to the bad news yet, but it was obviously about me.

I was the bad news.

And as it turned out...I was the one who couldn't handle it. That was the beginning of the end.

13

"The walls are done," Michael told me Monday afternoon. He and Dean had spent the morning at my house patching and filling the holes in the walls.

I'd been surprised to find them there when I went to visit Mr. Smith at the practice. They'd told me that since they owned the company, their crews worked the various projects, and they popped in where needed to provide supervision and assistance. That allowed them to take on my home themselves immediately, and I wasn't going to complain about that. I just hoped none of their crews were suffering in the meantime.

"You're going to want to wait about twenty-four hours before you start priming the walls," Mikey added. "Give the putty time to dry."

I nodded, looking around the space. The patched walls already made the house look better.

"We're pulling up the carpets now," Michael said. "Then we'll work on the ceilings. In fact, you'll want to prime and paint those, too, once we're finished."

"What can I do to help?" I asked, wanting to do something, even though I had no business doing anything of the construction variety. I also didn't have the time.

"Nothing; we got this, Jess." Dean assured me as he passed by with some carpet scraps in his gloved hands.

"There's a catalog there on the counter," Michael lifted his chin towards the kitchen. "It has different kinds of flooring...carpet, wood, and veneer. Take your pick."

Now that was right up my alley. I wandered into the kitchen and picked up the catalog. The pages were filled with different colors of wood, carpets, tiles, and linoleum. Looking around the cottage, I decided wood floors would be the way to go. I liked the idea of dark wood in the bedroom to go with the whiskey colored walls. Maybe a lighter wood for living area. Definitely tile for the bathroom and kitchen.

I spent another hour or so browsing and marking the catalog with my notes, then I checked my watch. I had five minutes until I was due to meet Mr. Smith in the office.

"I'm heading next door if you guys need me," I called as I slipped out the front door. They had finished pulling up the carpet and were busy taking down the doors. I was surprised at how quickly they were getting everything done, but it was a small place and most of the damage was aesthetic. I guessed it helped that they didn't have any furniture to work around, and literally everything was being renovated, so they didn't need to worry about damaging anything.

Hearing a vehicle approach, I looked towards the road. Mr. Smith pulled into the small gravel lot in front of the office and parked in the unmarked space beside my car. I'd briefly seen Mrs. Smith to pick up the key to the cottage the morning Mom and I checked it out, but Mr. Smith hadn't been home.

"Jessica," he said in his deep baritone as he got out of the car. "Dear girl, look at you!"

I smiled as I stepped into his open arms. "It's good to see you, Mr. Smith."

"None of that. Call me George," he held me out at arm's length. "We're peers now." I knew he meant it in the professional sense, but I still had to tamp down a giggle at the thought of a seventy-year-old man being my peer.

Mr. Smith looked good for his age. He was short and a little thick around the middle, but he still had a full head of thick, white hair and his eyes danced with youth. He'd always had an energy about him, despite his age, and I was glad to see that hadn't changed.

"I'll try," I said, following him up the brick steps to the small porch.

"Would you like to do the honors?" he asked, holding out the key.

"No, you go ahead," I waved him off. I never was one to make a big fuss out of stuff like that. Plus, I'd have plenty of time to celebrate my new office and job in the coming months when I was able to make the place my own. Right now it was still Mr. Smith's. For a few more days.

He unlocked the door and stepped inside, flipping the switch for the lights as he went. It had been so long since I'd been inside the practice, but it looked the same as I remembered. Four leather chairs sat in the small waiting room, and on the other side of a glass partition was the reception desk. Mrs. Smith had graced that desk for as long as I could remember.

I'll have to hire a secretary, I thought to myself.

Mr. Smith—err, George, that was going to be difficult—led me back to his office, which would soon be my office. I knew from our last conversation that he had a few cases he wanted to close up himself but would be handing the rest of them over to me.

"This cabinet back here," George patted the top of the black metal filing cabinet in the corner behind his desk, "contains all the active cases. Mostly property stuff, some family law, estates..." he trailed off. I could tell this was hard on him—leaving his life's work behind.

"I promise I will take good care of all your clients," I assured him, placing my hand on his forearm.

"I know you will. I know you will. The few cases I'm hanging onto are estates undergoing some modifications. Once those are complete, they'll go in this cabinet over here." He walked over to another black filing cabinet, neatly labeled "ESTATES." "Archives are in the file room," he gestured towards the closed door across the hall.

I nodded, taking it all in. Owning my own practice was going to be overwhelming...in a good way, of course. It hadn't completely sunk in yet that this was all mine, but I couldn't wait to get started and work on something other than employment contracts, which had been my job at the corporate firm in the city. I'd be happy if I never had to review another contract in my life.

"Occasionally I'll get contracts from some of the local businesses. Just basic review stuff," he added, bursting my contract-free bubble. "I have complete faith in you, Jessica."

It had been so long since I had felt pride towards myself, especially coming from another person, but I did in that moment. I hadn't had too much to be proud of lately. If I was being honest, I hadn't had much to be proud of since I graduated law school. That was my last major accomplishment after graduating high school, college, and then marrying my high school sweetheart. It all went downhill from there.

"Thank you," I finally said. "I can't wait to get started."

"Not much that's pressing aside from the Miller/Bostick property dispute."

"What's going on there?" I recalled the big Miller farm just outside the town limits near the rec fields, but the Bostick name was new to me.

"The Bosticks own the land adjacent to the Millers, what used to be Chester Cameron's place."

"The Camerons moved?" They were one of the founding families of Oak River. That news surprised me.

"Chester Cameron passed away two years ago, a year after his wife, Betsy. The kids weren't interested in the land and sold the place to Gerald Bostick. Big city guy who retired and wanted to turn the Cameron farm into a vineyard."

"Is the land right for that kind of crop?"

"Nope," George chuckled. "But he tries like hell every year."

I laughed with him. "So what's the dispute?"

George sat in the big leather chair behind the desk and sighed. Taking his lead, I sat at one of the guest chairs in front of his desk—my desk. It was still hard to believe this was my practice, especially with Mr. Smith here. He had such a commanding presence; I hoped the people in town would have the same faith in me as they had in him.

"Bostick has a big compost heap in the back corner of the property. Miller says the land the heap is on belongs to him. Neither party has been able to find paperwork or property maps that confirm or deny either claim."

I wanted to roll my eyes. Both farms had to be hundreds of acres, and they were arguing over what probably amounted to no more than a couple hundred square feet. But that was small town life. I wasn't in the "big city" anymore, and thank goodness for that. I had wanted the slow pace and low crime rate of Oak River. Speaking of crime...

"Any criminal cases?"

George raised his eyebrow. "In Oak River?"

I laughed. "Just thought I'd ask."

"I think I've had maybe a handful of DUI cases over the years, but that's about it. Not too much of that kind of thing happens in Oak River, and if it does, the public defender's office in Smithfield usually takes it on since it's free."

Smithfield was the county seat, holding the courts and the headquarters for law enforcement. It was where the local community college was, the train station, and shopping malls. Larger than our small town, Smithfield was still a small town itself.

Honestly, I was looking forward to the slow pace. Contract law wasn't all that urgent, but everyone in the city had been in a rush and seemed to wait until the last minute to get things done. I was always given tasks that were due the following day, and I didn't like constantly operating in emergency mode. Correction: I had enjoyed all the busy work when I needed to get away from my own thoughts, but once I started to find myself again, I found that it wasn't all it had been cracked up to be.

"If you don't mind, I think I'll hang out here today while the guys are working in the house and review some of the open cases."

"You don't have to ask my permission, Jessica. The place is yours."

Leaning back in my seat, I took another look around and sighed contentedly. Feeling that big swell of pride again, I smiled...it was mine. I could get used to feeling this good.

14

"Knock, knock." Michael's voice startled me. I lifted my gaze from the case file spread out on my desk and was surprised to see the sun had set outside the large bay window in the office.

"Gosh, I completely lost track of time," I said, stretching my arms above my head. My back cracked, and I made a mental note to find a chiropractor.

"I figured. We just finished cleaning up inside," he said, gesturing to the house. "The cabinets have all been sanded, too."

My eyes widened at that. "Already? You guys did all that today?"

"It's a small cottage, Jess," he smirked. "Your kitchen isn't much more than a galley. You've got like six cabinets."

"There's more than six cabinets in there," I said, defending my little home.

"Fine, seven."

I laughed, doing a count in my head. There were about ten cabinets total in the kitchen. "Is there a special kind of paint I should get for them?"

"I think it would look best with a light stain rather than paint, but you can do whatever you'd like. It would be great if you could get the painting done before we put in the flooring. We'll finish up the ceilings tomorrow, so I'd suggest painting on Wednesday."

"I think a stain sounds nice." I could go purchase the paint tomorrow morning and be ready to go Wednesday morning. "Would you be able to meet me at the hardware store to look at the stains?" It didn't matter how detailed his instructions were, I'd likely still purchase the wrong stuff. I was not Ms. Home Improvement...Danny had always handled that kind of thing around the house.

I was surprised that thought of him hadn't caused as much pain as it had only days ago. Maybe I *was* healing...finally.

"Sure. I can meet you there around nine, I have to drop by a job site first thing." The fact that my little brother had to take care of work "first thing" and would be finished with it in time to still meet me at nine was crazy. Nine o'clock was what I considered first thing in the morning, even when I worked at the firm.

"That sounds perfect. Thank you, Mikey."

"No problem. We should be able to pick up the flooring you picked out tomorrow or Wednesday."

"That's wonderful. I can't believe how quickly all of this is coming together."

He shrugged. "It's a small project, and you wanted it done fast."

"Well, it might be a small project, but it's still a lot of work. I appreciate it."

"Yeah, yeah," he waved me off. "You having dinner with the 'rents?"

"Nope," I answered, rising from my desk chair and stretching again. "They've got some meeting tonight so I was just going to pick something up on my way home."

"I'm heading to The Diner; want to join me?"

"Sure. Just let me put these files away." I made quick work of putting back together the handful of files I'd been reviewing.

Mr. Smith had been right. Nothing I'd come across was particularly urgent—mostly wills and estates that needed the occasional update when a new grandchild was born, or when someone pissed off a relative enough to get written out of their will. Some of the wills were quite entertaining. Gotta love small towns and big, crazy families.

"All right, ready," I said as I turned the key in the lock of the file cabinet.

Michael left ahead of me, waiting in the grass as I locked up. "Think you're going to be happy here, sis?" He asked as I joined him.

I looked at my new home and my new business, then at my brother and smiled. "I think I already am." I hooked my arm in his as we walked the rest of the way to our cars.

***

"I think you'll find a lot of what you're looking for at the flea market. They have a lot of rustic, repurposed things straight off of Pinterest."

I let out a small laugh. My buff little brother knew what Pinterest was.

"What?" he asked, pausing with a forkful of meatloaf halfway to his mouth.

I shook my head, "Nothing." I told him. "It's just a little funny that you know what Pinterest is."

He rolled his eyes and ate his food, waiting until he chewed and swallowed before continuing. Nothing but manners, my brother.

"I don't live in a cave, Jess. Mom's entire kitchen came off Pinterest. During the entire remodel, all I heard was 'Pinterest this' and 'Pinterest that.' Makes me glad we don't do residential work. With commercial jobs, the folks have ideas, but they're rarely that specific."

"Well, I honestly never even thought to consult Pinterest for ideas." It was true, but I sure was thinking about it now.

"Great," Michael said, glaring at me. "You've got that look now."

I laughed and speared a stalk of asparagus with my fork. "Just in terms of interior design, not carpentry." I remembered seeing one of those pallet-style headboards a while back. That would look great with the whole rustic feel I was going for.

"Well, just don't mention the word 'pallet' to me, and we'll be fine," he said, eyeing me.

I laughed; it was as though he was reading my mind. I tipped my glass of tea to him. "Deal."

"There's some new home store Mom and Karla were raving about at family dinner last month. It doesn't have furniture or anything, but it's got bed things, towels...that kind of thing."

"Oh yeah? I'll ask them about it."

I'd sold all my furniture in one big yard sale when I sold the townhouse, and donated most of the linens, knowing that the modern styles and designs wouldn't have matched the cottage. Hell, they wouldn't have matched Oak River with all their clean lines and sharp edges. The only big piece I'd kept was a small, wooden heart-shaped table Danny and I had picked up at a local artisan showcase shortly after we were married. I'd been so excited, it was our first handmade piece, and I'd had dreams of picking up more like it for our home. Never did get around to it. It was one of the many things I'd set aside in my pursuit for a family.

Thinking back to those days, I wondered when exactly I had stopped living our dream. The early days of trying to conceive were still optimistic. We whispered about baby names and shared secret looks, like we knew something the rest of the world didn't. After a few months, it became mechanical, but we were still optimistic, *I think.* Sure, the seed of doubt had been planted, but we were two young, healthy people. It would happen eventually— soon even—and when it did, the easiness of our lives would return. We'd smile and laugh like we used to, randomly tossing ridiculous baby names at each other, like Banana June or Maple South. We'd go back to fooling around for fun, instead of because it was a certain time of the month.

It hit me then, like a ton of bricks to the face.

God, I thought, *three years.* I wasted three years trying to have a baby. Ok, maybe all the years weren't a *total* waste, I mean we didn't know there was a problem that first year, but we should have. It should have been easier than it was, but it wasn't. That should have been the first clue. Why we waited an entire year to see a specialist was beyond me. Maybe things would have been different if we'd sought out help sooner. Or maybe they would have ended that much faster.

It wasn't that wanting and trying to get pregnant was a waste of time. That wasn't it at all. It was that I had an amazing, loving husband through all of that time. A man who wanted to share the burden with me, and I didn't let him. I wasted *that*. I wasted him. And I'd regret it for the rest of my life.

"Jess?"

I registered the mess on my plate before looking up at my brother. I'd apparently merged my asparagus and mashed potatoes while stuck inside my head. The look on Michael's face told me it wasn't the first time he'd said my name.

"Sorry, just thinking about stuff."

"You okay?"

I took a mental inventory and nodded. I was okay. It was getting less difficult to think about the past and what I'd lost. Many people don't think of infertility as a loss because there was nothing tangible to lose, but oh, how I grieved for the lost opportunities and possibilities. They were as real to me as anything. Having never actually gotten pregnant, I never knew anything more than that...opportunities and possibilities.

"I'm good," I said, smiling at him. For the first time in a while, it felt like the truth. It felt like thinking about the past was more therapeutic than painful.

"You mentioned you had all your colors picked out?" he asked, moving the conversation to something safe and comfortable.

"Yes. I'll pick up the paint when we go to get the stain in the morning."

We spent the rest of dinner talking about the renovations, and I welcomed Michael's opinions about the space. It was fascinating, listening to my little brother talk shop. He really liked the rustic charm theme, and he had a lot of ideas. It was almost as though he'd spent a lot of time thinking about it, and I wondered if he and Kara had dreamed of what their home would look like. We settled our bill—I insisted on paying for his meal, much to his chagrin—and we made plans to go to the flea market over the weekend with his truck.

Life was good.

15

I was back in the hardware store Wednesday afternoon, frustrated and sweaty; my clothes streaked with two shades of paint.

I'd managed to finish painting my small bathroom that morning, and then I made it halfway through the bedroom before the wooden extension pole for the paint roller Michael and I had just purchased snapped right in half. Yeah, I might have been applying a little too much pressure, but I was getting tired. Painting was no joke. Thank goodness I'd agreed to let Michael and Dean paint the ceilings with their fancy spray machine because there was no way I would have been able to hold the roller over my head to do that job. I rubbed my poor, sore arms. I needed to find a gym, stat.

I picked out a metal pole, smacking my hand against its length for good measure. I smiled at the inanimate object—it passed my silly little inspection—and turned away from the shelf to head to the cash register, almost running right into Danny.

"Whoa," he said, placing his hands on my arms to steady me. "Easy there, killer."

I found myself smiling at the odd endearment. He'd called me "killer" in the past often, when referring to my feisty side—in the most loving way, of course. Danny didn't know how to be anything but loving. I hadn't seen that feisty girl in a long, long time. Neither had he.

"You're not going to hit me with that, are you?" he asked, gesturing to the pole in my hands.

I looked down at it and absently shook my head. "Painting," I told him.

"Me, too," he said, holding up a pack of paint brushes.

I nodded. This was awkward. I didn't want it to be awkward. I didn't know what I did want it to be but awkward definitely wasn't it. We had too much history for it to be awkward, then again, it was *because* we had so much history that it *was* awkward.

I sighed, frustrated, but I made no move to leave. Being in his presence calmed my constantly racing thoughts. It wasn't like this when we ran into each other at the diner or even when I'd seen him at the bar. But something changed...at the park...the barrier I'd erected, the Danny deterrent, it was gone.

He lifted his hand and touched a lock of hair that had came loose from my ponytail. "I like the color," he noted.

I looked at the strand in his hand, my eyes widening at the whiskey paint streak.

Shit. He wasn't supposed to see that.

"It's my favorite color," I told him. *It's the color of your eyes,* I thought to myself. I didn't

102

say my thoughts aloud, but he knew. It's what I said when I chose the same color for the bedroom of our townhouse all those years ago.

Those whiskey eyes were brighter than they'd been the last few times I saw him. Less sad. It was as though my confession had given him a hope he hadn't had before. I felt guilty for that, but I wasn't sure why. I wasn't really sure what I was supposed to be feeling, or why I was supposed to be feeling it. I was so confused.

"Do you need any help?" he asked, surprising me. He looked like saying the words physically hurt, like acid on his tongue. Which is probably why I didn't shoot him down. I think I surprised him as much as I surprised myself when the next four words came out of my mouth.

"I'd love some help."

***

"Shit." *Shit, shit, SHIT!* What in the hell had I just gotten myself into? I just invited my ex-husband to my new home to help me paint my bedroom the same whiskey brown color as our marital bedroom...the same color as his eyes!

"Ohmygod. Ohmygod." I bopped my forehead against the steering wheel one, two, three times as I sat at the one stop-light in Oak River.

Why did I say he could help? What was I thinking?

I wasn't thinking. That was the problem.

No, that wasn't true. I *was* thinking. I was thinking that I couldn't bear to see rejection on his face one more time. I couldn't bear to see the pain behind his eyes. The moment he'd offered to help, I saw it. Quick like a camera shutter, that pain of his. It was there, like he'd forgotten who he was talking to for a moment and just offered some neighborly assistance, then he remembered and snap.

When I agreed...his eyes turned a shade of greenish-brown I'd never seen before. Well, that's not entirely true either. I had seen them that color before. On our first date. When we'd had our first kiss. Said "I love you" for the first time. Our first time making love. Our wedding day...

The fact that a tiny, insignificant moment of me accepting his help ranked up there with those once in a lifetime relationship milestones for him really said something about the way things had become between us. At the end of our marriage, I wouldn't have accepted Danny's help with the car door, so this really was something. A breakthrough of sorts.

But what did it mean?

Did it have to mean something?

I wished I could get out of my head. Just for one day.

I pulled into my driveway. Danny gracefully bought me some time, saying he needed to run home to change into appropriate painting gear. He'd been wearing ragged clothes at the hardware store, but I think he knew I needed a minute to process. Always considerate, always intuitive. They were two of the many reasons I fell so head over heels in love with him all those years ago.

"I'm so sorry I was late," Danny said, taking a seat in the booth beside me. He always did that, sat beside me instead of across from me. He said he wanted to be as close to me as he could. It was sweet.

"It's fine," I lied. I was pretty annoyed at him. It was our six-month anniversary, and we'd agreed to meet at The Diner at six o'clock. Didn't he understand how embarrassing it was to be a girl, all dressed up for a date, without her actual date? A few groups of kids from our high school had passed through The Diner, and they'd all seen me sitting alone. Some laughed, and I was certain it was at me.

I tried so hard not to cry. I always cried when I was angry, but I wouldn't do it now. Not over a boy.

He reached across my lap and placed his hand over mine. My skin felt hot under his. I swear there was even a sizzle.

"I really am sorry, Jess." He sounded so genuine… "Look at me, please?"

My eyes lifted from our hands to his pretty brown eyes. It was weird describing a boy's eyes as "pretty," but they sure were.

"I was on my way here when I saw Mr. and Mrs. Roberts walking down Main Street holding bags of groceries. Turns out their car wouldn't start in the parking lot and the auto shop was closed so they couldn't get it looked at or a tow. I gave them a lift home. I couldn't let them walk all the way home."

Mr. and Mrs. Roberts were probably the oldest people in town. They must have been in their eighties. They didn't live far from the center of town, but for two senior citizens, I didn't think the distance truly mattered. A block was too far for them to have to walk in the summertime, not to mention while carrying grocery bags.

"You did a good thing," I told Danny, forgiving him immediately and falling in love with him just a little bit more. He had such a genuinely good soul.

"It was nothing," he said, blowing off what he'd done. He always downplayed his good deeds.

"I love you, Daniel Andrew Thompson," I told him for the first time.

Those pretty brown eyes lit up like firecrackers on the Fourth of July. "I love you, Jessica Lynn Price," he said.

As his lips brushed against mine, I melted. I melted right into a puddle on that red vinyl seat.

I loved Danny, and he loved me. My life couldn't possibly be any better than it was in that moment.

16

"Come on in," I said nervously as I held the door open. Danny slipped by me, his shoulder brushing against mine ever so slightly. The light touch sent tingles through my entire body. I'd missed that feeling.

"Wow," he commented, taking a look around.

"I know," I said, trying to see what he saw. The main living area looked gutted with the concrete slab exposed, patched walls, and stripped cabinets. It was hard to believe this was actually progress and not the starting point. "It's rough," I added, feeling a little embarrassed.

"Nah, it's not that bad," he said, setting down a box of what appeared to be more painting supplies on the floor. "If you want to see bad, you should see my place."

"I'd like to," I admitted, surprising myself, and him, yet again. I'd always loved his uncle's property. The house was always just a house, but the land was beautiful.

"Yeah?" he smiled a crooked smile, and my heart skipped a beat.

I nodded, pleased I'd made him so happy twice in one day. Maybe I could do this friendship thing with him. Maybe.

"Well, all right then. So where are we working?" he asked, and I appreciated that he wanted to get down to business. He was probably as nervous as I was that we'd lose this easy...whatever it was...that was happening between us.

I'd thought about locking the bedroom door so he wouldn't see the unfinished walls, but he'd already seen the paint in my hair, so there was no use. "Well, I need to finish the bedroom," I said, pointing to the open door. "And this whole space is going to be that sage green color. Except for that wall," I said, pointing to the wall that was shared between the kitchen and living room. "That's going to be navy blue."

"Navy?" he asked, his lip curling.

Ahh...navy blue was one of the colors of Oak Ridge's rivalry school. Some things never changed...

I shrugged my shoulders. "I think it'll look pretty."

"Well, I don't know about that," he said. I would have been offended if I couldn't tell he was hiding a smirk on his handsome face. He pulled some painter's tape out of the box he'd brought inside and walked over to the far corner of the room. "How about I get started out here while you finish up in the bedroom?"

I felt myself relax. He was ignoring the whiskey-colored elephant in the room, er...house. Maybe it was just as curious to him as it was to me that I was painting my new bedroom that same color. Or maybe it was just too difficult for him to be in my bedroom with me, even without the bed. The bedroom *had* become a very unpleasant place for us. What was once a place of rest and fun had become all business. A chore. An angry space.

"That sounds great," I agreed and quickly disappeared into my bedroom.

***

Awkward...again. I'd just finished painting the last wall in the bedroom and was too scared to go out to the living room. I could hear Danny moving around the space, the beat of the country music he'd started listening to about an hour ago bounced through the walls.

"Hard to Love" by Lee Brice played, and the lyrics resonated. I had to have been hard to love, and yet the other day Danny had told me he *still* loved me. How was that even possible after I pushed him away? After I'd treated him like he was invisible. The most wonderful man in the world...

Get out of your head, Jess, I warned myself.

I straightened my big girl panties and walked out of the bedroom before I could convince myself otherwise.

"Wow," I said, coming to an abrupt stop.

He'd almost completed the three sage walls, and the room looked like an actual room.

"Amazing what a little bit of paint can do."

"You can say that again," I muttered, my eyes scanning the space, evaluating the work that remained. "Thank you so much," I told Danny as I brought my paint roller to the kitchen to dispose of the cover.

"It's nothing."

I hated the way he downplayed the work he'd done. He'd been like that for as long as I remembered, whether it was giving rides to senior citizens or painting his ex-wife's living room.

"It's not nothing, Danny. This is huge." I looked around the room. It would have taken me an entire day to do all this. "It's such a big help for me, and you didn't have to do it. You're..." I sighed. "You're something else, Danny Thompson."

He gave me a small, one-sided smile. Memories of when I'd first and last name him rolling through both our minds, I was sure. They were always good times. Happy times. Sweet times. Sassy times.

"I'll get started on the accent wall," I told him, looking away and breaking the silent moment...the staring contest between the two of us. Gosh, it had felt good to just look at him, to take him in again. He was still so damn handsome. Hot even. Yes, definitely hot.

He finished up that last sage wall as I started the navy one, and then promptly declared it was time for pizza. My stomach chose that exact moment to growl, so I couldn't exactly argue. He called in an order to the local pizza joint—ham and pineapple, my favorite—and left to pick it up after cleaning up his workspace. By the time he returned, I had finished the accent wall and was cleaning up. I was so glad Michael advised me on the paint with the primer in it because it appeared one coat was all I'd need. I'd be happy if I never had to paint again.

I cleared a space on the living room floor, spreading out a clean drop cloth for us to sit on. Danny set down the pizza, two-liter of Sprite, and a plastic bag containing paper plates, cups, and napkins. He'd thought of everything.

After pouring us each some Sprite, Danny held his cup up in a toast. I did the same, tilting my head to the side wondering what he was up to.

"To your new place," he said. "To new beginnings. I hope you find what you're looking for, Jessie."

I felt the familiar sting of tears, but I didn't let them fall. I wasn't quite sure what I was looking for...peace, happiness...but I sure hoped I found it, too.

"You too, Danny. You too."

The conversation stayed light after that. We ate our pizza and shared renovation stories. Mine weren't nearly as interesting as Danny's, but he was invested in my words like they were the most brilliant thoughts ever spoken. The common bond was nice, it took the pressure off our history...the past. And as he tucked me into my car at the end of the night, we made vague plans for me to come out and see his house. I wasn't sure I was ready for that, and he knew it, so he didn't push it.

"Good night, Jess," he said. The whisper of his lips against my forehead before he closed the car door felt like an illusion...one I felt all the way down to my toes.

17

A few days later, the house was finished and the movers delivered the contents of my small storage unit from the city. The entire process took about thirty minutes before I was sitting alone on my finished hardwood floors with a bottle of champagne and a package of cheap plastic flutes I'd bought specifically to celebrate this moment.

This anti-climactic moment.

Alone.

Moving my entire life should have been a bigger experience, no? The boxes the movers dropped off barely filled my small living room. The items I could unpack would take me a handful of minutes, but most of it had to wait since I didn't have any furniture yet. No tables for my knick-knacks or shelves for my books. Not yet.

Except that table.

I stood from my lonely place on the floor and walked over to the handmade table, carefully unwrapping the bubble wrap. The table's smooth surface was heart-shaped and it stood about waist high. The light stained wood matched the floors in the living room almost perfectly, and I wondered if somewhere in my subconscious I'd known it would.

I placed the small table beside the front door, so it would be the first thing I saw when I walked into the house, the last thing I saw when I left. In one of those boxes I had a pottery bowl Emma had made. I received it in the mail with the rest of my Christmas presents last year. I cherished that bowl, that little handmade piece of imperfect perfection. I'd place that on the table, use it to hold my keys or something.

Leaving the champagne and plastic cups on the floor, I lifted one of the boxes labeled "KITCHEN" and set it on the formica countertop. Once the guys were done with the work, I gave the entire house a good scrubbing, so the cabinets and drawers were eagerly awaiting their new occupants. I ripped open the tape and began the mindless task of unpacking utensils, dishes, and cups.

The kitchen was nearly unpacked when there was a knock at the front door. Part of me hoped it was Danny. I hadn't seen him around town the last few days, and we didn't exchange numbers so I couldn't get in touch with him if I wanted to. *Did I want to?* I wasn't sure, but the way my body came alive at the thought of him at the door told me more than my mind did.

I finger combed my hair as I hurried to the front door, kicking a few empty boxes out of the way. The sky was turning a beautiful shade of purple as the sun had begun to set in the distance.

I pushed open the front door, seeing several shadows through the opaque glass.

"Surprise!"

My mouth gaped open. My family—my entire family, sans the kids—was standing on my tiny front porch. My mom and Karla held gift bags, Melissa, Bryan, and my dad held casserole dishes of some kind. Michael held a plastic grocery bag.

"What's all this?"

"It's your housewarming-slash-unpacking party," my mother answered, as though it was obvious why they were all standing on my porch on a Friday night. "I figured you haven't fed yourself all day, so we brought over some food. And able bodies to help you unload."

"You gonna let us in or what?" Melissa asked.

I stepped aside. "Of course, come in. I'm sorry," I said, shaking my head. Shaking myself out of my little funk.

Karla silently picked up my party for one off of the floor and brought the bottle and cups to the kitchen. She unsleeved the plastic flutes while Bryan uncorked the bottle, and they poured the now room temperature champagne together. I didn't like champagne anyway, it just seemed like a necessary step. They passed out the cups.

"To Jessica," my dad began, holding up his glass for a toast. "We're so happy to have you home, to have our family together again. Your mom and I are so proud of what you've accomplished here, and we know you're going to take Oak River by storm."

I smiled, knowing it wasn't really possible for an attorney—or anyone, really—to take Oak River by storm, but appreciating the sentiment all the same. "Thank you, Daddy."

"Welcome back, sis," Michael added. The rest of the group echoed Michael's words, and we clinked glasses.

"Thank you all, so much. Your help over the past few days has been wonderful. I'm not so sure I deserve everything you've all done for me as of late, but I sure do appreciate it. I love you all. Thank you." I raised my glass to them, and we clinked again. Hugs followed, then everyone took a box.

As I laughed with my siblings, ate my mother's delicious food, and gave unpacking directions, I let my mind wander back to my first meal in my new house. My first toast.

Danny.

I hadn't thought about it at the time, that they were my firsts of those particular moments in the house. But it seems appropriate that those times were with him. In fact, the only shadow on this otherwise perfect turn of events was that Danny wasn't here with my family.

He should have been.

Our toes touched, played with one another. I giggled, always ticklish on my toes.

We laid naked, wrapped in a blanket on the living room floor, having just christened our new home.

Our home.

It was surreal. Danny and I were married, and we owned a house. We were doing grown-

115

up things, and despite my twenty-two years, I very much did not feel like a grown up. With Danny, I always felt like a teenage girl.

Young and wild and free.

He kissed my forehead, and I felt it all the way down to my toes. To his toes. To my toes that tangled with his toes. I hoped this feeling never went away.

I nestled deeper into his chest, burrowing into his warmth.

Safe.

Happy.

Loved.

Everything I ever wanted with the one man I'd always known would be my forever.

Before succumbing to sleep, my eyes zeroed in on the one thing I insisted we hang, even if we didn't do anything else. A small wooden sign over the front door that read "and they lived happily ever after..."

18

Everything was coming together. Between the house and the practice, I was finally feeling like I found my place. That I fit into my place.

I was at The Bar. Correction, everyone in town was at The Bar. It was Mr. Smith's retirement party. He and his wife were leaving on an RV trip in the morning. They had children and grandchildren spread out around the United States and decided to take a tour of the country while visiting their family. Mr. Smith— George, I'd never get used to calling him that— promised I'd be able to reach him by cell phone if I needed anything, and I assured him I would call him at the first sign of trouble, knowing it would be unlikely that I'd ever be that desperate. I knew I had to give the sweet man peace of mind, though, and I would be forever appreciative of his faith in me. I knew he'd given me glowing recommendations to all his clients over the last couple weeks.

"If I remember correctly, you know how to throw a mean dart." His voice...his warm, minty breath...so close to my neck caused every single hair on my body to stand up on end. It was both exhilarating and concerning, being so close to him again.

I slowly turned, taking a step back, knowing if I hadn't, our lips would have—could have—brushed against one another. That's how close he was.

I looked into his brown eyes, seeing the little bit of challenge there. I used to know how to throw a dart, that was true. I couldn't tell you how the game was played, but I could shoot some bullseyes. I hadn't tossed one in years, but how hard could it be?

I smirked, letting him know his challenge was accepted. Making my way to one of the dart boards, I nodded hello to a few of the folks I passed. I'd been back in town three weeks, so I'd pretty much run into everyone by now. A few of them stared; Danny and me together in public was fodder for the gossips. I was okay with that, there were certainly worse things.

I picked up six darts, handed three of them to Danny.

"You ready to get stomped, Thompson?"

He grinned at my playfulness. It had been years since he'd seen the fun, competitive side of me. It was years since *I'd* seen her.

"Are *you* ready to get stomped, Price?"

I saw the light in his eyes falter ever so slightly. Calling me by my maiden name hurt him. He didn't let it sway him though. With my nod, he winked, then turned to the board. He readied himself, aimed, and fired.

Bullseye.

He'd been practicing...

He threw his second and third darts, also bullseyes.

Well.

I raised my brows, acting nonplussed, but I was shaking in my boots. Literally. I had on a denim skirt, pink and green plaid button down sleeveless top, and cowboy boots. But back to the darts...Danny had never been that good. Sure, we never played the right way. We just threw to see who could hit the bullseye. I hadn't thrown in years, and he was acting like he'd thrown every day for the last four years.

I cockily approached the line and threw. And I hit the wall.

The *wall.*

I, Jessica Lynn Price, never hit the wall.

"It's been a while," I mumbled.

I tipped my head to the right, then to the left, stretching my neck. Then I stretched my arms out to the sides and went up on my tiptoes to stretch my legs...I was stalling. He knew it, I knew it, the wall knew it. Maybe I needed another beer. I looked at the dart in the wall. Then again, maybe I didn't.

I stood at the duct-taped line on the floor again, lifted my arm, pulled back, and tossed the dart.

Into.

The.

Freaking.

Wall.

Again.

I stood there, blinking. For real?

I glanced at Danny. He was trying not to laugh, covering his mouth with his hand—the nice guy that he was.

"What the heck, Jess?" Michael bellowed, coming up behind me.

I shook my head, I honestly didn't know. It was no secret I was a dart hustler back in the day. Not here at The Bar because I wasn't old enough to be here before I left town, but in our friends' garages, basements, and game rooms. There wasn't much to do in a small town so we had a lot of house parties. Most of us had dart boards and pool tables. The pool tables were always hogged by guys *teaching* girls how to play, so I threw darts.

Evidently, I'd lost that skill.

And apparently I'd drawn an audience. Thank you, Michael.

I lined up again, hell bent on making this next shot. I felt Danny behind me, my body coming alive from his proximity.

"Just take it easy," he said, his voice a whisper. "The dart is just an extension of your hand."

I looked over my shoulder at him and sneered. "They teach you that in coach school?" I asked.

He laughed. A few people around us laughed, too. Probably thankful that Danny and I were in each others' presence, and it wasn't awkward. It was about damn time it wasn't awkward. Things in Oak River might be okay after all, they probably all thought, secretly celebrating.

I pulled my arm back, threw the dart.

Bullseye!

I shrieked, bouncing and clapping my hands like I'd just won the lottery rather than gotten a one out of three on our fake little game. People around me cheered, excited simply because I was excited. I spun around, trying to find Danny.

He was there. He was always *right* there. He wrapped his arms around my waist and lifted me in the air, spinning us around in circles. It was an exaggerated celebration of nothing, but I reveled in the closeness. Mostly because it didn't hurt. Being close to him like that didn't hurt. It felt like old times, and I loved the nostalgia.

Danny let me down and released me. I felt his absence immediately, but was distracted by the high fives of our friends and neighbors. It was ridiculous, celebrating one lousy bullseye so emphatically, but it was more than that, I thought.

It was a reunion. A welcome home and a bid farewell. A celebration of new beginnings and old goodbyes. It was a genuinely good time. A Friday night in a small town.

I let myself wonder for a few moments...why was it I'd been so desperate to leave this place? Why didn't I ever want to come back?

Oak River wasn't so bad. I caught Danny's eye across the room and he smiled—one of the smiles he reserved only for me. I felt my face flush, my body full of awareness. No, Oak River wasn't so bad at all.

19

I hung a left, my car bumping along the dirt drive that led to Danny's uncle's place. Well, it was Danny's place, now, I supposed. He really needed to even this driveway out if he expected my little car to make this trip ever again.

Getting ahead of yourself? the little voice of reason inside my head asked.

The voice was right. There was no sense in anticipating any return trips. Danny and I might be getting along fine, but we'd resolved nothing. We hadn't had one conversation about our past, and that was okay. We hadn't seen each other in years, and we were getting reacquainted. We were both back in Oak River to stay, so we had plenty of time to rehash the past.

I pulled to a stop in front of the barn. Looking at the big red structure, I wondered if Danny was planning on having any animals. His uncle had horses, but that was years ago. I didn't think anyone in Danny's family had livestock anymore. I was stalling again.

I opened my car door and stood, stretching my legs. We all closed down The Bar the night before. Thankfully, I didn't drink the entire bar like I had with my siblings when I'd first gotten back into town, but I was up late, and my body was letting me know it wasn't thrilled. I stretched each arm across my body as I took in the landscape.

It was so beautiful. So green. I could see why Danny would have wanted to rebuild his life here. So much potential. So much promise. There were so many things that had been lost between us that he could find here, *with someone new*. The thought was like a stab in the gut, and I almost bent over from the pain.

I'd never considered Danny moving on, but he could have. If not already, then in the future. We were divorced. We were nothing to each other. Maybe friends. Maybe not. I didn't even know. He said he loved me, but maybe it was a friendship type of love. The kind of love people always have for their first loves. A sentimental kind of love.

I took a deep breath, trying to calm my raging thoughts.

"Hey," he called out. I jumped, the shock of hearing his voice jolting through me. "You okay?" he asked, his boots crunching on the gravel as he approached.

"I'm fine," I lied, giving my best smile. It was bullshit and he knew it but, bless him, he didn't say anything else about it.

"All right," he said. "Let's grab the four-wheeler and I'll give you the grand tour."

"I've already been here. You don't have to give me a tour."

"Entertain me, will ya?" he asked, that signature crooked smirk present on his handsome face.

How could I say no?

He slid open the heavy barn door, his biceps flexing underneath his tight white t-shirt with the exertion, and then disappeared inside. A minute later, I heard the loud motor of the ATV start up. He drove it out of the barn and pulled up alongside me. He held out his hand and I took it.

Of course, I took it.

I'd always take it.

"Isn't your uncle going to get mad?" I asked Danny as we snuck into the barn on his uncle's farm. It smelled of hay and something sour, probably horse pee. His uncle had a couple horses somewhere around here.

"He's out of town at the rodeo."

I followed Danny blindly through the dark, my hand gripping his. He'd been here a million times before. I trusted him to lead me through the dark.

He sat atop something and pulled me right up behind him. We were on a four-wheeler. The loud engine made me jump when he started it. I swear it would have woken up the town if we weren't in the middle of nowhere.

Danny rode out of the barn and across the field, the small vehicle breezing through the night. The ATV's headlight gave him just enough light to see where he was going, but I knew he knew those fields by heart. He didn't need directions or a map, he could probably feel his way with some kind of farm boy sonar.

After a few short minutes of my arms wrapped tightly around his waist and the wind whipping my hair behind us, we stopped. Danny climbed off, then helped me. I saw the moon's reflection on the river and smiled. I knew exactly where we were.

"You took me to the river?"

"Yeah...thought we could cross something off that bucket list of yours."

I blushed. My bucket list was ridiculous, a silly journal assignment for my composition class. It included things like dancing in the rain and skinny dipping. My blush deepened...he wanted to... "You want to go skinny dipping?"

He smirked at me, then pulled his shirt over his head.

"I don't know," I said, looking around nervously. It wasn't that I thought someone would see us, it was more that I couldn't see what was in the water...or the field... "What if there's an animal or something?"

Danny kicked off his shorts and started making his way down the short dock. "I didn't know you to be a chicken, Jessie," he taunted.

When he reached the end of the dock, I could barely see him in the moonlight. He looked over his shoulder, still grinning at me as he pushed his boxer briefs down his long, muscular legs. The sight of his white butt made me giggle. He was all tan, except for his butt.

"Are you laughing at me?" he asked.

I nodded, grinning like a fool, forgetting his taunting words and my fear of the unknown; I just wanted to be with him. I started peeling my clothes off, and I watched his Adam's apple *move as he swallowed. The way he looked at me...I felt cherished.* Empowered. *Like I was the only girl in the world. The most beautiful girl in the world.*

I ran down the dock and grabbed his hand. He gave me a quick kiss before we jumped off the end.

I forgot about the imaginary creatures in the river and the monsters in the field. All I thought about was the guy in front of me, holding me like he was never planning on letting go. I melted into him, letting him carry the weight of me...of everything.

- 20 -

"The river is pretty dried up," Danny said, pulling me from my memory.

I looked ahead of us, over his shoulder and felt a deep sadness run through me. The dock we'd jumped off of as kids was there, but the water line was at least fifty feet beyond that.

I reluctantly released Danny's waist and climbed off the four-wheeler. We walked down the dock, our booted footsteps sounding hollow without the water below. I paused at the end, seeing an image of us in the water under the moonlight. Him holding me, so close and so tight.

Oh, to be seventeen again.

"Uncle Pete said there were several dry summers. Water level dropped each year. Sad to think it may completely dry up one day."

The thought almost brought tears to my eyes. Aside from the night we skinny dipped, we'd come to this river a lot that summer. Kicking our feet off the dock, swimming around, floating on our inner tubes that were connected to the dock by a rope so we wouldn't float too far away.

The fact that it had dried up just like our relationship...it hurt. It hurt a lot.

As though he knew I needed the support...the feel of his touch...Danny put his arm around my shoulder and pulled me into his side. *Always so intuitive.*

"We had a lot of good times here," he said, reading my mind.

"We did," I agreed, staring out across the expansive space. The tree line across the way seemed so much closer without the water running in between.

"Are you looking forward to starting work on Monday?" He dropped his arm from my shoulder and sat at the edge of the dock, legs hanging off the end, feet swinging.

I copied his move, sitting beside him. "I am. It's kind of weird," I confessed. "I don't have any appointments or anything, so I have no idea what the day will bring, but I am looking forward to getting up in the morning, getting dressed and walking all the way across the driveway to my office."

"Do you miss the city?" he asked.

I frowned. How to put it into words? Simply... "No, I don't miss it."

"That's surprising," he said, glancing at me briefly. "You loved it so much."

I sighed. As easy as our camaraderie was, there would always be the hard parts. The tough parts. The real parts. They would always be there until we talked about them, resolved them, and they weren't there anymore.

"The city wasn't kind to me," I said after a while. I must have surprised him with my reply because suddenly he was looking at me with a curious expression on his face. "I had so many hopes and dreams, you know? Plans for city life. It all came crashing down around me. Maybe it was my own fault, but it happened all the same."

"Jess, none of what happened was your fault," Danny said. The honesty of his words shown through his light brown eyes.

"Wasn't it, though?" Maybe it wasn't my fault that I'm infertile. Maybe that was God or biology or Mother Nature or whatever, but wasn't the way I handled it my fault? Isn't that what ultimately caused our downfall?

Danny sighed. He knew me well enough to know that was a rhetorical question, and that the old argument still stood. I held the weight of the failure of our relationship, of our future, on my shoulders. Therapy and time wasn't going to change that. His words weren't going to change that. It was up to me. I had to change my mind, and I wasn't quite ready to do that. I wasn't there yet.

"We did everything we could, but the damage was irreparable. We had to remove both of your fallopian tubes." The doctor's words echoed in my head long after he'd spoken them.

"It'll be okay. We'll get through this," Danny said, and I nodded absently. I looked away from him and towards the window of the post-surgical unit, not really seeing anything. I noticed the sky was gray, which was the way my heart felt. Gray, drab, dreary.

My chances of conceiving a baby—Danny's baby—naturally had just gone out that hospital window.

What kind of woman was I? Was I even a woman if I couldn't perform this one task? We were biologically made to carry children. I had all the right parts; they just didn't work. I felt like a failure. I was a failure.

I was incomplete...literally...having just had my tubes removed due to an old inflammation. Some kind of bacteria had caused damage to my tubes and ultimately resulted in a blockage that couldn't be fixed. Was I naïve to have thought they could repair it? I didn't think so before, but now? Not so much.

I felt useless.
I felt like less of a woman.
I felt like nothing.
Nothing.
Nothing.
Nothing.

That had been my second chance. My second chance to make a better choice, to react differently. To fall into my husband, instead of away from him. Another lost opportunity.

"Come on," Danny said, patting my leg. "I want to show you the house."

We got on the four-wheeler and headed back towards the barn. The ride back was quiet and less fun than the ride out. I didn't hold on quite as tightly as I had before, it just didn't feel like I should. A heavy silence hung over us, one that was my fault. I always had to go and make things uncomfortable.

I followed him across the driveway towards the large two-story farmhouse. It was painted red to match the barn, but I'd always imagined it would look more welcoming in a robin's egg blue. He brought me in through the mudroom and we kicked off our boots. The kitchen came next, it was large but under construction, so it was impossible to determine how it would look when it was complete.

"How do you cook in here?" I asked, running a fingertip along the dusty granite countertop.

"I've been getting most of my meals from The Diner and from my mom."

"What would we do without our parents?" I asked, realizing how ironic that statement was coming from me.

"They've been my rock," he admitted.

"Mine have been really good to me since I've been home."

"They would have been there for you before, too, you know?"

I turned away from him, frustrated. Why did he have to bring that up? Things were already weird enough between us.

"I guess I just don't understand, Jess." His voice was angry, bitter even. "After all this time, why you're back. Why did you choose to come home now? Why did you choose to accept help now? Why couldn't you have done that while we were together? When we still had a chance?"

Each one of the words stung, like a whip lashing at my back. So did the insinuation. *When we still had a chance,* as in we didn't have a chance now. I honestly never expected a second chance with Danny, but the finality with which he spoke those words was cutting. It broke open a wound inside me I thought had healed or that at least had scabbed over. Maybe there had been hope. Some little seed of hope I hadn't even known I still held.

Keeping my back to him, I walked to the front door.

"Oh, that's real rich, Jessica. Walk away when it gets hard. I guess some things never change."

Now that pissed me off. I turned around and glared at him. "Is this why you asked me here, Danny? To get me away from prying eyes and on your turf so you could tell me how you really felt about me? Huh?"

He had no answer for that. He looked surprised I was saying anything at all. Well, some things did change. Just because I wasn't prepared to rehash our painful history didn't mean I had no fight in me.

I shook my head at him. "And for the record, Danny, I'm not the one who walked away. That was you."

As the front door slammed behind me, I knew what I said had been a low blow. I knew damn well he wouldn't have walked away four years ago if I hadn't have made him, but he pushed my buttons, and I pushed back.

The feisty "killer" Jessica was back. I hoped he was ready for her.

21

I spent the morning in the file room at the office, scanning paper files onto my newly purchased server. The IT guy for the newspaper helped set me up with a small network so I could work on bringing the practice into the twenty-first century. I paid him for his time and promised to use him in the future for follow-up freelance work. He and his wife just welcomed their third child, and he told me he could use all the extra money he could get.

It wasn't until my ex-husband came in the front door carrying something that smelled delicious that I realized I was working straight through lunchtime.

"What are you doing here?" I asked him. I wasn't about to be pleasant. His behavior at the farm yesterday still bothered me, warranted or not.

"I come bringing gifts. A peace offering," he said, holding up a small house plant and a greasy paper bag. My traitorous stomach growled. "This is a cactus," he said, placing the plant on the reception desk.

"I know what a cactus is."

"And this is lunch," he said, ignoring my snappy attitude and waving the white paper bag like it was a flag of surrender.

I raised one eyebrow and waited. If he wanted to apologize, he was going to have to say it. Then maybe I'd consider apologizing for my part in the argument.

He set the bag on the desk and sighed, running both hands through his hair. *Oh boy.*

"I'm sorry, Jess." He paused and looked around briefly. "It used to be so easy for us, you know? All this trying stuff? It's hard work. I'm still a little mad at you. And hurt. You gave up on us. You just gave up. That wasn't the girl I knew. *You* weren't the girl I knew. I mourned her loss for years. I mourned liked you'd died. I was lost for a long time before I finally found my way back home. I went through the motions in the city, finished my teaching contract, my master's, then I came back here. And then there you were. And it was like you're her but you're not. And I'm still mad at you. Sometimes I don't know if I ever won't be mad at you. Other times I realize I was never truly mad at you at all. Just hurt. I don't know what to do with all that. Regardless, I shouldn't have confronted you like that at the farm. I didn't mean to ask about the city. I knew if I had, I'd go there, and I really didn't want to go there. I didn't mean to go there. So for that, I'm sorry. But I'm not sorry for feeling. I'll never be sorry for having feelings."

I wiped the tears from my eyes, grateful I'd caught them before they spilled down my cheeks. "I'm sorry for what I said. I know it was a low blow."

He just shrugged. "I deserved it. It was actually kind of nice to see you fight back, even if it stung...and was a bit misplaced."

I winced. I was tired of hurting him. I wished everything could just fix itself, but I wasn't quite ready for that yet. In order to move forward, to get past it, he would have to understand that I blamed myself, he'd have to accept that. And I didn't think he ever would, not fully. He could blame some things on me, but he wouldn't place all the blame on me... It just wasn't in his genetic makeup.

"I accept your apology, if you accept mine."

"Apology accepted," he said, and his easy smile was back. "Can we eat now? This smells amazing."

"Of course," I said.

We each pulled chairs to the reception desk and Danny began unpacking the bag from The Diner. He had brought foil wrapped burgers and french fries, a diner classic. Greasy, but delicious.

"So how has your first day been?" he asked.

"Not too bad. Sort of boring, but I'm getting things done and that's what's important. One day I may be too busy to be able to take care of some of this administrative stuff, so I'm going to appreciate the free time while I have it."

"Will you hire a receptionist?"

"Eventually. Seems silly to do it now though, when I barely have enough work to do myself."

"Are you scanning stuff?" he asked, looking around at the piles of papers everywhere.

"Yeah, I'm creating electronic files."

"Good idea," he said, nodding his head.

I smiled, feeling validated for something that I was vaguely afraid was a waste of my time. "Thank you."

He smiled in return, and we finished our meal with some small talk about his parents and their plans for retirement.

"I can't believe your dad is going to retire," I said. His father had been a deputy sheriff for as long as I could remember. He worked for Smithfield County, but his jurisdiction was Oak River. He and a handful of others dotted our small police force. The crime rate was so low in Oak River, the job was probably a cake walk.

It's no wonder he'd remained on the force for so long.

"I know, it's weird. I think he's going to end up driving Mom crazy after just a few weeks."

I laughed, picturing Mrs. T throwing Mr. T out of the house. "Your mom was always a force of nature."

"She still is. She'd like to see you, you know? You should go by the house."

I frowned and poked at my fries. "She doesn't hate me?" I found myself asking. Maybe I hadn't meant for the words to come out. Or maybe I had. But I'd always wondered. Dean didn't have a problem with me, but that was Dean. I hurt his brother, not his son. The term Mama Bear was coined specifically for Mrs. T. I wasn't going to lie, I was afraid of the woman. I was afraid of her as a teenage girl dating her son, as a woman married to that same son, and now as her son's ex-wife. I was also surprised I hadn't run into her or Mr. Thompson in town yet. Or maybe I was lucky...

"Hate you? She could never hate you, Jess. Mom loves you. She misses you."

I blinked.

"Don't look so surprised. She always adored you. You were like the daughter she never had."

"But she has a daughter."

"Yeah, well Darcy doesn't count. She drives my parents crazy."

"Still?" I asked, remembering his little sister as a wild child. She'd wanted out of our one-stoplight town more than I had. As much time as I'd spent with the Thompsons, I hadn't spent a lot of time with Darcy. She was never around. Always taking off to here or there with this guy or that guy. She probably single-handedly kept the Smithfield County Sheriff's Office in business in Oak River the year she ran away from home six times.

"Yeah. She lives in California now. That's where Mom and Dad have been. They took a few weeks off and headed out to visit her. I think this trip is a trial run of Dad's retirement. See if they can put up with each other," he laughs.

I smiled, remembering the easy banter between Mr. and Mrs. Thompson. I did miss them, I was a part of their family for a long time. Knowing she didn't hate me...didn't blame me...it was like a weight had been lifted, one I didn't even realize I was carrying. I guess maybe I'd thought they were avoiding me this week, too, so it was a relief to hear they were actually just out of town.

"I'd love to see your mom. I'll make it a point to stop by this week."

"She'd like that," he said, finishing off the last of his burger. He looked at his watch. "I've got to get going, I have practice in a few."

"Isn't it the off season?" I asked, trying to ignore the way the muscles in his arms flexed as he cleaned up his trash.

"It's never the off season, Jessie," he said. Repeating what he always used to say when we were kids. Football players worked as hard, if not harder, in the off season than they did during the season. Couldn't get soft now, could they?

"Thanks for lunch," I said. "And the company."

"Anytime, Jess." He winked as he walked out the door.

Gone just as quickly as he'd appeared.

If I didn't have half a burger, some fries, and a cactus in front of me, I'd almost claim he had been just a figment of my imagination.

22

"You do realize anything else you buy today will have to go in your lap?"

"Aw, come on, Mikey. We can pull some *Tetris* style maneuvers and fit at least one more table in there."

"There's already four tables in the bed of my truck. Need I remind you that your place is not all that big?"

"Two end tables for the living room, a dining table, and a night stand. Nothing wrong with any of that," I said, hoofing it down another row packed full of amazing items. I also picked out some mismatched chairs for the kitchen table and a variety of decorations. The truck *was* pretty full, Michael was right to be concerned.

"What else could you possibly need?"

I stopped so abruptly, Michael bumped into my back. "You might be right..."

"Can you say that again?" he asked, holding his hand up by his ear so he could hear better.

"Shut up," I said, smacking him in the gut. "I may have gotten a little excited and carried away considering this is my first trip out." We started walking again.

"I'm just surprised you don't have a list."

I tapped my head. "I have tons of mental notes."

"How do you remember everything?"

"I don't know. It's always been easy for me." I didn't have an eidetic memory, I just didn't forget things. I had an innate ability to organize ideas in my head, like one would organize to-do lists and piles of work on a desk.

"Well, I could use someone with your brain at the office. I swear Shelley is the most incompetent person in Oak River."

"Shelley Moore?" I asked, and he nodded. "She was a twit in high school. Why did you hire her?"

"Her daddy runs one of our crews, asked for a favor."

"And now you're stuck."

"And now we're stuck," he agreed.

I didn't need my years of HR law experience to know that was a bad idea. Never do "favors" in the workplace. Especially when it involves a job—a crucial job at that. But Mikey didn't need my lecture.

I picked up a piece of recycled metal art, trying to figure out what it was.

"You like dolphins?" a big, bearded man asked from behind the table.

I looked at the little sculpture in my hands. I did like dolphins, but this didn't look like a dolphin.

"I prefer land animals," I lied, smiling at the man and setting the hunk of junk down on the table and quickly moving on.

Some of the flea market folks seemed like okay people, others were creepy as hell. Metal Guy fell into the latter category. His stained white overalls oddly reminded me a little too much of the butcher apron that dude wore in *The Texas Chainsaw Massacre.*

"I heard Dan brought you lunch this week."

I rolled my eyes. Stupid small town. "Who told you that?"

"Dean."

Should have guessed. Danny was pretty close with his brother. "Didn't know you guys gossiped." I passed by a few more stalls of handmade crafts. Nothing stood out. Maybe I was all shopped out. Was that a thing?

"Is it gossip if it's true? Or if it's family?"

"It's gossip until you know it's fact," I said, not even sure if that was a thing, but it sounded like sound gossip logic—which sounded like an oxymoron.

"I know it's a fact. I may have also seen him at your office."

"What?" I asked, turning to face him now. "Why were you there?"

"I just happened to be driving by."

Note to self: You have absolutely no privacy in Oak River. Especially when you live right off Main Street.

"Well, it was nothing," I said and continued weaving through the booths. "He brought me lunch. An apology for pissing me off."

Michael's tone darkened. "What did he do to piss you off?"

I looked over at him, surprised by his tone. I'd never witnessed my little brother act protective on my behalf before. Or at all, for that matter. Being grown up looked good on him.

"It was nothing," I shrugged, downplaying the argument Danny and I had at the farm. "We just have a hard time being around each other and remaining civil."

"Seemed pretty civil at The Bar for Mr. Smith's party."

"Well, we go from day to night pretty quickly. It's easy to fall into something comfortable with Danny. Then we remember we got divorced for a reason, and that reason hasn't fully been resolved yet."

"So what are you waiting for?"

I reached the end of the row and stopped, stepping to the side and looking up at him. "What do you mean?"

"Resolve whatever it is that needs resolving," he said, crossing his arms over his chest.

"Michael, it's not that easy," I laughed.

"Sure it is."

"No, it's not. There are years of damage."

"But you still love him."

My eyes filled with tears. "It's not enough," I said, my throat thick with emotion. I was going to cry. Right here in the middle of the flea market. "Can we please just not do this right now?" I asked, wiping the corner of my eye.

He softened, putting his arm around my shoulders and pulling me into his side. "I didn't mean to upset you, Jessie. You're both still so stupid in love with each other, I just don't get why you won't work it out."

Because Danny deserves so much more than me.

"I hurt him pretty bad," I confessed. "It'll take a lot more than a Band-Aid to fix us."

"Jessie," he moved to look into my eyes. "You may have hurt him, but I can assure you, that man doesn't care about any of that. He still looks at you like you hung the moon and all the stars. You probably wouldn't even have to apologize."

I laughed. *If only.*

"No, I'd definitely need to apologize."

"So do it," he pressed. "You know what I would give to have one more moment, one more second, to understand why she left? I'd give my life for that chance. You don't even have to do that. You can just walk up to the guy, say you're sorry, kiss and make up."

I frowned, looking past Michael, focusing on his truck out in the parking lot. I hated that my brother was right, and I hated his pain over losing Kara even more. But regardless, Danny deserved a lot more than me. He deserved a family and someone who could give him that.

"Maybe you should let him make the decision."

Had he read my mind? Or had I said that last part out loud?

"You said you hurt him," he continued when he saw my puzzled look. "Sounds like he should be the one who decides whether or not he forgives you, not you."

Right again, Mikey.

The thing was, I was pretty sure there was nothing left for Danny to forgive. It wasn't a matter of forgiving really, it was a matter of talking. It was a matter of me telling Danny every thought and every feeling. Exposing him to my darkest thoughts, laying myself out bare. I wasn't ready for that.

"Let's go," Michael said, tugging me towards his truck. "I want to grab some pie from the farmer's market on the way back and it shuts down at two."

My laughter was light, but my heart was heavy...my mind on Danny, as usual.

23

One evening after work, I decided to walk to The Diner for dinner. On the return trip home, I took a detour down Magnolia Lane. It wasn't an unconscious decision. Danny's parents lived on Magnolia.

I paused at the curb and looked up at their modest ranch home. The brick was still the same bright red it was when we were children, hadn't dulled a bit. His mother had loved the red brick and got so angry at us kids when we took our sidewalk chalk to the side of her house. We'd spent as much time pressure washing it as we had committing chalk crimes.

The memory reminded me of just how far back my history with Danny went. Our lives had been intertwined since we were in elementary school, before that even, I just didn't remember that far back. I remembered being in the same class from kindergarten through third grade, and getting so upset when we were placed in different classes for middle school. We'd grown apart during those years, boys had cooties and all that, then reunited in junior high. He certainly didn't have cooties then. I crushed on him so hard until he finally asked me out sophomore year.

My eyes moved from the low window of Danny's childhood bedroom—one I snuck in and out of more than a few times—to the wide expanse of grass where so many pictures were taken. Memories made. Smiles had. We took our prom photos under the tree beside the driveway. I ran up the perfectly straight flagstone walkway to show Danny my college acceptance letter. We walked down that same walkway together, hand-in-hand, the night we'd told his parents we'd gotten engaged.

I was staring down at the rock path, so I didn't see Mrs. Thompson open the front door. I didn't see her walking down the walkway until her slipper clad feet were in my line of sight. My eyes darted up to her face, surprised at her sudden appearance.

"Oh, my dear girl." She gave me a sad smile and pulled me in for a hug.

It wasn't until I was in her arms that I realized I was crying. "I'm sorry," I said, not really knowing what I was apologizing for in that moment. For crying? For breaking her son's heart? For not coming to see her sooner?

"Why don't you come inside? I just boiled some water for tea and there's some leftover pie."

I let her lead me into the house, wiping my eyes as I walked. I still didn't know what to say to her. What was a woman supposed to say to her ex-mother-in-law?

The house smelled the same as it did years ago, and a new wave of nostalgia washed over me. Memories of being part of the Thompson's family dinners flashed through my mind. Big, raucous meals that occasionally ended in food fights between Danny and Dean. Sometimes Mr. Thompson was involved as well. When the food went flying, Mrs. T would always calmly get up from the table, having faith that the boys would clean up the mess. And they always did. Those boys hated upsetting their momma.

"Sit," she said, nodding towards the kitchen table. I did as I was told, operating on autopilot, it seemed. She handed me a warm mug and sat down on a chair catty-corner to me, then stirred some sugar into her tea. The house was so quiet, all I could hear was the hum of the refrigerator. It was nerve wracking. Mrs. Thompson was a big woman, and I didn't mean her weight. She had a large frame—tall with wide shoulders—and she was intimidating as hell.

"You look like you're about to pee your pants," Mrs. Thompson said, seeming to read where my thoughts were going.

"I just might," I admitted.

She laughed, and I couldn't help but laugh, too. Mrs. Thompson had that kind of laugh— boisterous and infectious.

"It's good to see you," she said with a sad smile.

"It's good to see you, too."

"Don't lie," she joked.

I smiled. "No, really. It *is* good to see you. I hadn't realized how much I missed everyone, every*thing*, until I got back here."

"It's good to have you kids home again," she said, looking down at her tea. "We missed you both so much while you were gone. Greg and me, your mom and dad, your brothers and sister, Dean. I even think Darcy missed you guys. That girl..." she trailed off.

"I'm so-" I started to say, but she interrupted.

"Don't apologize. We understood. You two needed to go conquer the world in your own ways."

"But we should have come home more," I said, disappointed in myself.

"Yeah, you should have," she sighed. "But that's in the past. You're here now."

"You don't hate me?" I couldn't help but ask.

Mrs. Thompson tipped her head to the side and looked at me with confusion on her face. "Why on earth would I hate you?"

"Because me and Danny…"

"Went through some things no one should ever have to go through. My gosh, sweet girl, we hurt so much for the two of you."

"But-"

"But nothing, Jessica Lynn. I can't pretend to know exactly how you felt after being dealt blow after blow like that, but I know a thing or two about loss, about grieving, and I know how painful and all-consuming it can be. I didn't share this openly before, and maybe I should have been more open about it, maybe it would have allowed the two of you to be more open with us, and maybe things would be different. It took Greg and me a long time to get pregnant with Daniel. We tried for years, went through what seemed like a million tests. There was no known cause. I got pregnant four times, each ended in miscarriage."

My heart sunk for her. "I'm so sorry."

"I don't know what changed with Daniel," she continued. "He must have been as stubborn an embryo as he is a man, because he stuck, and we had a healthy baby boy. Six long years after we'd started trying to have a family. Dean and Darcy came easily, too. It was like a switch had flipped, I guess. I'm not telling you this as one of those 'never give up' stories, I know how annoying they are, and I heard my share of them all those years ago. I'm just sharing this with you, woman to woman, a mother to a daughter. I would have loved to have been there for you when you were struggling. I'd love to be here for you now."

A tear dripped down my cheek. For her loss, her pain, and her love. After all this time, after my history with her son, she still considered me a daughter.

"I broke Danny's heart. How can you still…"

She smiled sadly, placing her hand over mine. "Honey, you didn't break his heart. My son is still so in love with you. You can both be as stubborn as you need to be right now, but you'll find your way back to each other eventually."

Why did everyone keep saying that?

"We got divorced," I said, as if that explained everything. It was the end of our story, was it not? The period at the end of our sentence. The final nail in the coffin. People didn't come back from divorce…did they? Could they?

She shook her head, that *I know something you don't know* look in her eyes. "You two never fought as kids. Never had an argument. Your relationship was easy in high school and college. It was picture perfect. The stuff people write romance books about. You created a perfect world for yourselves where all your dreams came true. You loved and loved and loved, but it was all you knew how to do."

I frowned, unsure I liked the picture she was painting. Danny and I hadn't been completely naive to the world around us, had we?

"There's nothing wrong with the way things were. It's wonderful that you two were able to enjoy each other for so long without arguing about this, that and the other thing. Your struggles with infertility were the first big, grown-up problem you had. Your first conflict. Neither one of you knew how to handle it. Now, I see that look on your face," she said, calling me out on my furrowed brows. "I'm not trying to patronize you. It's just a fact. No one knows what to do in situations like that, they just get by. Neither you nor Daniel are guilty for what happened, but you never resolved your issues.

Don't let your first real fight be what separates you forever."

She patted my hand, then stood from the table and went to where a pie rested on the kitchen counter. She busied herself with cutting the dessert, but I knew what she was really doing. She was giving me time to process what she'd just said.

Was it true that Danny and I had never really fought before we started trying to conceive? Was that the root of all our problems? We just didn't know how to deal?

24

Mrs. Thompson set down a plate with a slice of warmed apple pie on the table in front of me. I thanked her, picked up the fork, and began eating. She excused herself from the kitchen, something about laundry. I barely paid attention, stuck in my own head.

I picked through my memories of mine and Danny's relationship, from when we'd been friends as young children to the very beginning of our romantic relationship in high school, and all the way to the end and our divorce.

Sure, we'd gotten a little ticked off at one another here and there, but we never really fought. Not until we started trying to get pregnant.

I remembered the first time.

"Honey, I'm home!"

I sprung up from the couch at the sound of Danny's goofy greeting and ran to the front hall to see him.

"Whoa," he said, smiling as I practically threw myself at him. "Not that I mind the enthusiastic greeting at all, but what's the occasion?"

"I'm ovulating!" I cheered.

"That's great, babe," he said, taking off his jacket and kicking off his shoes. I reached for the button on his jeans. "Hey," he said, stopping my hands.

"What's wrong?" I asked, frowning up at him.

"I just walked in the door, Jess."

"So, can't we be spontaneous?" I gave him a flirty smirk.

"Yeah, we can be spontaneous," he said, smiling, but still holding my hands. "But it's not really spontaneous when you tell me you're ovulating and then want to have sex."

"But there's a very brief window of opportunity each cycle-"

"Yeah, I know," he said, interrupting me. "You've told me every month for the last six months about that very small window. I get it, Jess. But I just walked in the door. I've been sitting in a horribly boring lecture for the past three hours, and before that I was teaching all day. Is it so much to ask that I'm able to come home a chill for a little while?"

"But-"

"I'm hungry," he said, ignoring me and walking towards the kitchen.

"Danny...this could be it."

"I read stuff online. There are blogs and articles that say we should just relax and let things happen naturally. They say that trying too hard can bring on stress and make it even more difficult to conceive."

I read those same articles. I hated them. I got that same advice in the online baby groups I joined. Relax, it'll happen. *The biggest load of bullshit I'd ever heard.*

He opened the refrigerator and pulled out the plate of baked chicken I'd saved for him. He pulled off the plastic wrap, ate a cold string bean, then put the plate in the microwave to reheat.

"Look, I think we should take a step back."

"Take a step back?" I echoed, physically taking a step back, away from him. "But we want a family."

"I know that, Jessica."

"Do you not want to have a family anymore?" I felt tears prick behind my eyes. Was he changing his mind? Was it my fault because I wasn't pregnant yet? We'd been trying for almost a year.

"Of course, I do," he said, stepping around the kitchen island and pulling me into his chest. "I want nothing more than to have a small army of kids with you. But it's gotten so mechanical, Jess. There's no romance. No love. It's becoming a chore, a duty."

"Making love to me is a chore?" I asked, pulling out of his grasp.

"That's not what I said. And we're not even making love anymore, Jess. It's like a damn science experiment. We're trying all these positions because you read that they were good for some stupid reason or another. There's no sweet talk or dirty talk, it's like you're directing the scene. 'A little to the left. No, not there.' It's exhausting. Is it so much to ask that we just have fun? People get knocked up all the time by just having fun. Can't we try that?"

Every word that came out of his mouth was like a stab directly into my heart...into my womb. Exhausting. Directing. *Was I really that terrible? That* mechanical?

"I'm sorry I've ruined our sex life. But if you recall, we were just having fun, as you put it, and nothing happened! That's why I've started using the ovulation predictor kits and-"

"See? That! Ovulation Predictor Kits. That's not sexy, Jess."

"You're right, Danny. It's not sexy. It's life. It's our life. It's what we have to do."

"But we don't have to do all that. Can't you see? You want to do all that. But we don't have to. We can just let it happen naturally."

"But it wasn't happening naturally!" I screamed.

He stared at me, open-mouthed. I'd never yelled at him before. He didn't know what to say or do. Hell, I didn't know what to say or do. I turned away from him and ran up the stairs to our bedroom. He didn't call after me, he didn't follow me.

I laid on our bed and waited. He never even came to bed. In the morning, I found him asleep on the couch with a pillow and blanket from the linen closet. So he hadn't even just accidentally fallen asleep on the couch, he'd planned to sleep there.

My heart cracked.

What was happening to us?

"Hey there," Danny said, bringing me back to the present.

I looked to the kitchen doorway, surprised to see him. "What are you doing here?" I asked.

He smiled that crooked smile. "Well, seeing as though this is my mom's kitchen, shouldn't I be asking you that question?"

"Probably so. I was out for a walk and stopped by to say hi to your mom. Your turn."

"Mom texted me a few minutes ago, saying that she had pie. Now I'm pretty sure it was a set up."

I knew it was a set up. I put a forkful of pie in my mouth. "It's delicious."

He cut a slice of pie for himself and sat across from me at the table. "Did you two have a nice visit?" he asked.

"We did," I said, smiling.

"Will you have dinner with me?" he asked next, surprising me with his boldness.

"Like a date?"

"Yeah," he said, nodding. Then he frowned. "No, not *like* a date. An actual date. A real date."

I looked down at my pie. "I don't know, Danny."

"Please, Jess. Just think about it. You don't have to answer me right away. Promise you'll think about it?"

His brown eyes looked so hopeful, I couldn't help but nod. "Yeah, I'll think about it."

His answering smile was big, but it didn't reach his eyes...his eyes remained cautious. "Thanks, Jessie."

We continued to eat our pie in silence, and I didn't refuse when he offered me a ride home.

Progress. We were making progress.

25

"I'll see you tomorrow!" I called from the front porch as I stepped in my front door.

Mom and Melissa had just dropped me off after a day of shopping and pedicures. I lugged my seven—yes, seven—bags inside the cottage and dropped them unceremoniously on the living room floor. I wasn't sure I had enough room for all this stuff, but there was a sale and you can never have enough soft towels and sheets, right? And blankets, and kitchen gadgets...I was so screwed. I didn't have the space for this shopping problem I seemed to have.

I reflected on my totally awesome day as I kicked off my shoes by the front door. I had such a fun time with my mom and sister. Yet another reminder of what I missed out on while I lived in the city. I'd also narrowly escaped the third degree about Danny thanks to Melissa's quick wit and ability to distract our mother with pretty, shiny things. Danny and I were hot Oak River gossip since we'd been seen around town together a handful of times. If Oak River had a gossip magazine, the headline would have read: *Would Oak River's golden couple get back together?* That's what they'd called us as teenagers...the golden couple. It was entertaining being the center of attention back when everything was sunshine and rainbows. Not so much anymore.

Deciding on some water and a pre-dinner snack, I headed for the kitchen. I stepped onto the tile floor of the kitchen and paused.

Squish.

That wasn't right.

I looked down and saw that my entire kitchen floor was soaking wet.

"Shit! What the hell?"

I grabbed some old hand towels from a drawer in the kitchen and threw them on the floor. It was no use though, the floor was completely soaked. I wasn't sure where it was coming from, but I guessed the sink. Thankfully it hadn't reached the wood floor yet.

Damn it.

I dried my foot off as best I could with one of the sopping wet towels, then went to my purse for my phone, which was on the floor in the living room, buried amongst the shopping bags. *I really do not want to have to use my new towels on this mess.*

I dialed my little brother and waited as the phone rang three times and went to voicemail. "Damn it, Mikey." I left a desperate message, "Mikey, I need you! Water everywhere! Help!" and hung up.

I looked at the mess on the floor and groaned. I had two bath towels that my mom had lent me. They weren't brand new. Surely, she wouldn't mind if I used them...I mean, I'd wash them...she wouldn't even have to know where they'd been.

I pulled the towels out of my tiny linen closet and spread them out across the kitchen floor. There, that took care of that. I wasn't going to pretend I knew what I was doing when it came to whatever was causing the leak, so I planned to ignore the kitchen until Michael returned my call.

I was almost finished unpacking my loot when there was a knock on my front door. *Yes, thank you, Mikey!*

As I pulled open the front door, I said, "Oh, am I glad to see you!"

"Likewise, Jessie."

It was *not* my brother.

"Danny? What are you doing here?"

"You mean you aren't glad to see him?" Dean asked, smirking beside his brother. I hadn't even noticed him there. Danny outshined pretty much anyone, even his mini-me younger brother.

"I'm so confused."

"Mike called me," Dean said. "You have a leak?"

"Yeah," I said, gathering my senses. I stepped aside and let them in. "The kitchen floor was soaked when I came home."

Dean headed into the kitchen while Danny hung back. "It looks nice in here," he said. He hadn't been here since he helped me paint.

"Thank you. It's coming together," I said, wringing my hands. I was nervous, and I wasn't sure why. I'd been alone with Danny recently, and we were currently chaperoned by his younger brother who was the biggest cockblock when we were teenagers. There was absolutely nothing for me to worry about.

"Bad news," Dean called out. I turned towards the kitchen. He was halfway under the kitchen sink. "We'll need to completely replace the pipes under here. I don't think we missed this crack when we did the walk through, my guess is it just happened from the stress of being used after all this time. I don't have the equipment to do that tonight. It'll have to be tomorrow."

I sighed, wanting to yell out *Why not?* "Okay, well, thanks for looking."

Dean maneuvered out from under the sink. "Don't use the sink until we can fix it. Or the dishwasher. The dishwasher draining through the sink pipes could have caused this mess."

"I did turn the dishwasher on before I left this morning."

"Just don't run it again and you should be okay. I'll get the stuff from the hardware store in the morning and come back."

"Are you sure? It's Sunday."

"Do you want to be able to use your kitchen?" Dean countered.

"Yes," I said.

"Then I'll see you tomorrow."

"Thank you, Dean." I laid my hand on his forearm.

"You're welcome." He looked at Danny, then walked towards the front door. "I'll wait for you in the car."

What?

Danny watched Dean walk out, then turned back to me. "Do you need help cleaning up?"

"No, I can manage. Thank you, though."

"You're welcome," he said, looking anywhere but at me. His hands were tucked into his pockets. He didn't want to leave, I could tell. I wasn't sure I wanted him to leave, either. But I knew he couldn't stay. I knew I wasn't ready for that.

"You should probably go," I said, then cursed because I sounded like a bitch. "I'm sorry, I didn't mean it like that," I said, looking up at him, his expression was pained and my heart broke. "I just meant that Dean is waiting for you."

He nodded. "Yeah. I should go." He sounded hurt, frustrated even. Why couldn't I stop hurting him?

Stupid, Jessica.

He turned to leave, and I put my hand on his shoulder.

He froze.

I froze.

What was I doing?

I didn't know.

He turned around, and he'd turned into my touch, so my hand was still on his shoulder. He was so close. He smelled so good.

This was Danny. The only boy/man I ever loved. Probably the only one I'd ever love. What was I doing?

What was I waiting for?

I took a step closer, closing the distance between us and putting my other hand on his other shoulder. I leaned my forehead against his. "I don't know what I'm doing," I confessed, and it felt good. It felt good to be so honest with him.

"Me either," he said. "But I like this." He put his hands on my waist. It was like we were dancing without moving. Our thoughts and hearts tangling with one another while our bodies stayed very much separate. Very still. As if we'd both spook if we moved.

Maybe we would have.

I closed the rest of the distance, crossing my arms behind his neck and resting my head on his shoulder. I hugged him. I breathed him. I loved him.

"I've missed this," he said. "Missed you." His voice was so quiet, as though he was afraid he'd scare me away.

"Me, too."

Then the horn honked outside.

"Fucking Dean," he cursed. Moment broken, he took a step back. "I'm sorry."

I smiled and shook my head. It wasn't his fault. "I'll see you around."

He nodded, returning my smile. He leaned in and gave me a kiss on the cheek. "I'll see you later."

I closed and locked the door behind him, then leaned my back against it. I took a deep breath, catching the lingering scent of him and sighed. He smelled the same, after all these years. I touched the warm spot on my cheek where he'd kissed me.

I wasn't going to be able to resist him for much longer.

26

My reprieve from twenty questions and opinions about me and Danny was short-lived. The following day I was at my parent's house with the rest of my siblings for Sunday dinner, and it seemed that everyone had something to say about us, even Karla who rarely said anything to anyone about anything.

"I always thought you two were the cutest couple," she'd admitted while we were setting the table together.

I always thought she and Bryan were the real town golden couple since they never actually left. The disqualifier was that Karla's family moved to Oak River her senior year, so she wasn't considered an Oak River kid. The joke was on Oak River though, considering Bryan and Karla were the couple who made it—did the whole family and white picket fence thing—right there in Oak River.

"Dean said you two were looking pretty cozy the other night," Michael added.

Then why did he blow the damn car horn?? I wanted to ask. I didn't, though, because I didn't want to draw additional attention. Not that the word "cozy" hadn't elicited questioning looks from Mom and Melissa. It did. *Damn him.* Michael had *such* a big mouth.

"George Malone mentioned he saw you two at the store together a few weeks ago. Buying paint supplies?"

I gaped at my father. *Seriously?* Since when was my dad in on the gossip? Or Mr. Malone, the owner of the hardware store. Dad looked properly chagrined, stirring his fork around his mashed potatoes, like even he hadn't realized what he'd said.

"There's nothing going on between me and Danny," I lied through my teeth to my family. I was probably going to be struck by lightning on the way home. Just fantastic.

Melissa snorted, the brat. I couldn't wait until I had some dirt on her. She would pay for her betrayal.

"Would it be such a terrible thing if there was something going on?" Mom asked. Her tone was innocent, but her intent wasn't. I might have been thirty years old, but it was still weird talking about my relationship, or lack thereof, with my parents at the dining room table. Especially with my niece and nephews at said table. Their wide eyes were volleying back and forth between whichever adults were speaking at the time, a conversation that was way above their level of understanding.

"I didn't say that," I said.

"Gwen said you stopped by the other day," she added.

"It was nice to see her."

"She said the same." She looked at me, as if questioning whether I'd elaborate on my conversation with Danny's mother.

Not here. Not now. I hoped I could convey that through my eyes. If they only knew, this type of inquisition was one of the reasons I had stayed away all these years.

"How's it going with the new town hall in Smithfield?" Bryan asked Michael, effectively moving the conversation away from my non-existent, yet tense love life. I sent him a small smile of thanks, to which he nodded in acknowledgement.

The boys talked shop for a while. Bryan's architecture firm designed the town hall Michael and Dean's company was building. My siblings were doing amazing things—they were happy—and they didn't even have to leave Oak River to do them. Most of all, they'd had each other all these years.

I wouldn't send myself back to *that* place again. I couldn't change the past, only the future. I was in Oak River now. I was part of the togetherness with my family now. That was what mattered.

"The Fall Festival is coming up. Are you attending?" Karla asked me while the guys continued to talk about framing and insulation.

The Fall Festival was a big deal in Oak River, right around the time the leaves began to turn beautiful shades of yellow, orange, and red. It was held in late September, shortly after school started back up, and sort of kicked off the fall season. The festival always took place on a Sunday, not to interfere with Friday or Saturday night lights—high school or college football. Oak River didn't care much for professional sports; we were all about our local teams though.

"Yep. I'll actually have a booth there," I told her. It would be my first attempt at marketing the firm. If I was being real, it would be the first time I'd be marketing *myself* since that's what it was all about in a small town. It wasn't the place or the thing, it was the person, or people, behind it.

"Oh," she said. "I didn't know that. I'm on the planning committee this year. No one told me."

"I actually just signed up on Friday, so it probably hasn't made it down the pipeline yet."

"It'll be great to have you there. And the sponsorship monies go straight to charity. This year it's a childhood cancer foundation."

"That's so wonderful. I love what this year's committee has done with the event," my mother added. She looked at me, shaking her head. "Last year, Lorraine Duncan was in charge, and she made an absolute mess of things. She completely forgot to include activities for the children, even though the committee mentioned it a number of times. People were so disappointed."

"Well, I'm looking forward to it," I said. "It'll be nice to have the opportunity to put myself out there, maybe drum up some work."

Honestly, I was so bored at work. My job was perfect for George—an older man ready for retirement—because it was so incredibly slow. But for me, someone who was accustomed to running at eighty miles per hour, it was too slow. I had wanted the change of pace, sure, but there was one day last week where I literally sat at my desk all day making a chain of paperclips that stretched from one side of the office to the other. That couldn't be my career. It just couldn't. I aspired to do much more than that.

"Things slow at the practice?" Dad guessed.

"Yeah," I admitted. "I'm sure part of it is just that people need to get comfortable with Mr. Smith not being the go-to attorney anymore, and part of it is that small towns aren't exactly active in the legal department."

"You should look into online consulting or something." Bryan's suggestion intrigued me.

"What do you mean exactly?"

He shrugged. "A lot of professionals are doing freelance work through the internet these days. A couple guys from my firm do consulting work. People send them plans or ideas and they give feedback. They don't take on the full job, but they give their professional opinions and get paid for it. My guess is there's a market for legal consulting...particularly on the internet since that way you can widen your audience beyond just Oak River."

"That's actually a brilliant idea," I said.

"Well, thanks. I do have them occasionally."

"Uh-huh." Karla mumbled.

"Babe," Bryan said, looking at his wife with his hand held dramatically over his chest. "You wound me."

"You'll be just fine," Karla said, not skipping a beat as she continued to eat her meal.

"Mommy, why did you hurt daddy's heart?" Luke asked.

Karla rolled her eyes at her husband's dramatics and leaned over to quietly address her five-year-old son's question. I had to stifle a laugh when I heard him ask his mother what "dramatic" meant.

27

Lightning did not strike me on the way home from my parents' house that night. But it might as well have since I was struck with both good and bad thoughts on the short drive to my cottage.

The common denominator?

Danny.

In one moment, I wondered if it was possible for us to start over. The next moment, I remembered one of the many times we fell apart.

"We still have one more embryo we can try," Dr. Rowland offered, but even he didn't sound optimistic.

"We've tried three. If the third one wasn't a charm, what makes you think the fourth one will be?" I asked. My tone was bitter. I was over this appointment. I was over this process. I was just over it all.

"Jess," Danny scolded, placing his hand on my shoulder in an attempt to what? Calm me? Console me? It wouldn't work. I shrugged him off. I was so sick of his optimism and positivity. I wanted to shout from the rooftops, "Why me?" But that wouldn't get me anywhere.

Nothing seemed to get me anywhere.

It was hopeless.

I was hopeless.

"Take some time to think about it," Dr. Rowland suggested.

I ignored his words as I stood from my stupid wingback chair and collected my coat and purse.

"Jess," Danny pleaded. "Jessica."

I ignored him, too. Him and his stupid super sperm.

I walked out of the office and out of the building, never planning on setting foot back in that house of false hope again.

I had been so fucking optimistic the first time I walked in those doors. I thought that place would hold all the answers. Problem or not, I was certain the fancy doctors would be able to fix it—fix me—and all would be right in the world. The truth was, it didn't matter how much of my inheritance I'd spent.

I was defective.

"Jessica," Danny called after me as I made my way to my car. "Will you wait a minute?"

I stopped walking and let him catch up. I wanted to cry. For the first time since all this started, I wanted to cry. But I wouldn't do it. Not in front of him. I couldn't let him see me break. I couldn't let him see how deeply this affected me. He wasn't an idiot, he probably knew, but I wasn't going to show him.

"Baby, it'll be okay. We'll figure it out." He took me into his arms and held me close.

I let him hold me and said nothing.

There was nothing we could do.

I was nothing.

Nothing.

Nothing.

Nothing.

The memory was bitter. If we thought we'd still had a chance back then, we were wrong. That was the real end. The point of no return—when I had officially shut Danny out. I stopped smiling. I stopped talking. I stopped praying. I just...stopped.

He never did though. Danny never stopped. He gave one hundred percent until the very end. He went to work or to class, and he'd always come home with a smile for me. He would kiss me on the forehead when he came or went and quietly sighed when I just sat there...nearly catatonic.

I remembered pieces of those days, but I was hardly able to paint a full picture. It all blended together. I spent a lot of days just staring off into space. I watched mindless reality television shows, not fully paying attention to anything that was happening on the shows or around me. I didn't even know what Danny had done those days. What he did when he was home. I never saw him. He could have been right in front of me, and I wouldn't have seen him.

Those thoughts...those memories...were why I was certain we would never work out. He must have harbored so much resentment towards me. What I saw that day at the farm was nothing. He must have had so much more to say to me. Right? I mean Danny was always perfect, but he wasn't *that* perfect, was he? So perfect that he'd completely forgive me?

He did seem to forgive me, though. The way he held me. The way he'd kissed my forehead. It felt like not a day had gone by. There was also the fact that he'd flat out told me he still loved me. That was no small thing. But you could love someone and still not forgive them, right? You could love them and still be so hurt from whatever it was that they did?

Part of me wanted to drive straight over to the farm and throw myself at his feet, begging his forgiveness. The sane, logical part of me drove straight back to the cottage and tucked myself into bed.

Alone.

The way I was destined to stay for the rest of my existence if I didn't just forgive *myself* already.

Danny had told me countless times that it wasn't my fault. The infertility wasn't my fault. I understood that and that wasn't exactly what had me tied up in knots. My reaction...that was my fault. My actions. My rejection of Danny was all on me. *That* is what I had a hard time forgiving myself for.

He'd been my everything. I took him for granted. Maybe some selfish part of me thought that no matter what I did, he would always be there. He always was there...even before we were a couple...for as long as I could remember.

Until he wasn't.

I laid in bed that night, restless, thinking of Danny. It was the place my mind always wandered to when I wasn't careful. I thought about the what ifs and the could have beens.

But most of all...most of all I just missed Danny. I missed him so much.

28

A few weeks passed, and I'd only seen Danny a handful of times in passing. In a sense, it felt like we were taking steps backwards. We'd had little moments here and there and then periods of nothing. I knew he was busy though. The school year had begun, as had football season. I may have gone to the first two home games. I hid pretty high up in the stands so he wouldn't see me, but I was sure he knew I was there. Word would have traveled down the bleachers that I'd been there.

Maybe space was what I needed though. Absence made the heart grow fonder and all that. Not like my heart could possibly have grown any fonder of Danny. It was maxed out with love for him. Always had been, and I knew it always would be.

I manned my booth at the Fall Festival. The weather hadn't turned bitter cold yet, so I was comfortable in a short sleeve button-down shirt and jeans. Karla worked some magic and arranged for my booth to be right beside the newspaper booth, so I had Melissa and Dad right next door. Some of the other staff came by to trade places with them throughout the day, but as the owner and the owner's daughter, they stuck around.

The sun was beginning to set; the air getting a slight chill to it. I had a beige cardigan in my bag that I slipped on after my third shiver. The smells of deep fried goodness floated through the air, and I itched for a funnel cake.

"How's it going?"

His voice sent a new set of shivers down my spine. Good shivers.

"It's going," I answered, smiling up at him. He looked incredible in dark jeans, boots, and a green and white button-down plaid shirt. The green in his shirt brought out the green in his eyes.

"Can you break away from here for a little bit?" he asked. He looked like he was up to no good, and I could never resist *that* Danny.

"I actually think I'm going to wrap things up."

"Can I help you with anything?"

I unceremoniously swiped my arm across the table, sliding my business cards and the informational brochures I'd spent the last week working on into a box.

"All done," I stated.

He laughed. "You don't have to take this down?" he asked, tapping the tent pole with his hand.

"Nope. The committee provided the canopy, table, and chair." I stood up, and before I could pick up my box of paper goods, Danny had it in his arms.

"Where am I bringing this?"

I nodded behind me. "My car is right back here."

A stretch of Oak River's Main Street was shut down for the Fall Festival. Vendors arrived early enough to get the good, close parking spaces. I was parked right beside The Diner, which happened to be right behind my booth.

I led him back, weaving through the people still lingering around. When I got close enough,

I pressed the button for the trunk on my key fob.

"Thanks," I said as he placed the box in the trunk.

"No problem." He closed the trunk and turned to me, his elbow sticking out.

I felt my cheeks go warm at the sweet gesture, then I wrapped my hand around his arm. "Where to?" I asked.

He just smiled and led me towards the center of town. I smiled nervously as people looked at us. They were *all* looking at us, specifically at where my hand held the crook of his arm.

"Don't even think about it," he said as I began to pull my hand away. "Let them think. Let them talk. We'll just be us, okay?"

I looked up at the man I loved. "We'll just be us," I repeated.

He smiled a million dollar smile and led me straight onto the makeshift dance floor in front of a small stage. A country music band crooned a cover of Alan Jackson's "Red on a Rose" and I melted into Danny's arms.

"Did you talk to a lot of people today?" he asked as we swayed slowly to the song.

"Yeah. Most were just people coming by to say hello, but I stayed busy earlier in the day."

"Good. That's real good."

His arms were around my waist, mine were around his neck, and my head rested against his chest. The position was the same one we were in the other night, and I felt like I was right where I was meant to be.

"Yeah. I'd really love to pick up some new clients."

"You will. I have no doubt. You draw people in, Jessica. In no time at all, you'll have this whole town hooked on you."

Like you're hooked on me? I wanted to ask. Would that have been too presumptuous?

171

Probably not, but it would have sent a message I wasn't ready to deliver. I didn't feel like I'd ever be ready, but I had a feeling Danny would wait. I had a feeling Danny *was* waiting. For me.

I sighed.

"What is it?" Always perceptive...

"This is nice," I said. It wasn't what I'd been thinking, but it was true nonetheless.

"It is," he said. I felt him press a kiss to the top of my head. So familiar.

I closed my eyes, remembering dancing in this same way many times before. Homecoming, prom, our wedding...

"I'm going to love you, every day for the rest of my life."

"I love it when you whisper sweet nothings in my ear," I smiled.

"There's nothing 'nothing' about it," he said, nipping at my ear.

The music changed from something slow to something fast, but we didn't pay attention. My head rested against his chest, his hands around my waist. He held me so close, so tight. I felt so safe, loved, happy.

It may have only been our senior prom, but I knew this was it. Danny Thompson was my forever guy.

"I love you, Danny. With all my heart and soul and everything else I can't possibly think of in this moment."

He pressed his lips to the top of my head, and I smiled.

"Every day for the rest of my life," I said quietly.

The brief pause in his movements and the tighter grip on my waist let me know he'd heard what I'd said. It let me know he remembered, too. When he held me a little tighter and rested his chin on top of my head, I knew he was as much at a loss for words as I was.

29

"What's going on with you and the older Thompson boy these days?"

I stared blankly at the elderly woman sitting in one of the matching brown leather guest chairs at my desk. She was the *third* client this week who felt the need to pry about my relationship. Apparently my public appearance with Danny at the Fall Festival over the weekend meant it was officially open season for relationship advice and opinions and everything else I didn't care to hear about.

"Mrs. Blakeney," I said, pointing to the documents on the desk, trying to redirect her attention.

"It's a damn shame you two split up. Kids these days," she started, shaking her head and tsking at me. I think some spittle landed my desk. "You all don't work hard for anything anymore. You just give up. That's not what a relationship is all about." She droned on, but I checked out, biting my tongue so hard I could taste blood. It wasn't the old bitty's fault she didn't know what she was talking about.

"And that sister of his," she continued. "It's a shame what she put that family through over the years."

"Mrs. Blakeney," I interrupted. She startled, looking at me with wide eyes. I might have raised my voice. Just a little bit. "If you could just sign here and here, we'll be all finished."

She wisely didn't say another word and signed beside the flags on both revised copies of her last will and testament. I thanked her for her business and walked her to the door, wishing her a good rest of her day before locking the door behind her.

I sighed and sagged against the door frame. What was with people? I don't remember the town being this invasive when I was in high school. No one seemed to care about Danny and me being together until we weren't anymore.

I scanned and filed Mrs. Blakeney's new will, then locked up my office. I didn't bother heading home to change, just got into my car and drove over to The Diner to meet Mel for dinner. I beat her there and slid into a booth, browsing the menu I had memorized at the age of seventeen. It never changed. There was just something about looking at a menu for the billionth time.

"Sorry I'm late," Melissa said, dropping her messenger bag down on the booth seat and sliding in across from me.

"I just got here myself," I told her, setting the menu down.

"Why do you even bother?" she asked, gesturing to the menu.

I shrugged. "Maybe something different will pop out at me. I don't know."

"It's all in the nightly specials," Melissa said. "It's what keeps things fresh. Mrs. Harper always has something new and different as a special."

The waitress came by and we ordered our drinks and the special, which was some kind of fried pork chop smothered in heaven. I could feel my arteries readying for the assault, but I didn't care.

"How's your story going?" I asked. She had mentioned she was working on an exposé piece about an entrepreneur who had been looking to purchase some land just outside of town.

"It's going," she answered, sipping the Coke the waitress just dropped off.

"That good, huh?" I asked. I squeezed a lemon wedge into my water and set the rind back on the saucer.

"He's just so...I don't know. It's hard to get any solid leads. He's very elusive is all."

"That's frustrating."

"Yeah, well, not as frustrating as your week apparently." I'd texted her earlier in the week after busybody number two had come into the office. Lawyer-client privilege didn't allow me to tell her who the clients were, but I could anonymously bitch to my sister.

"I wanted to think that they were making appointments because of the Fall Festival, but now I'm thinking they were making appointments just to meddle."

"It's quite possible."

"I just wish everyone would mind their own business. It's not like I don't put enough pressure on myself or anything. Let me just add all of Oak River to that."

"Just ignore them. I always do."

"What do they say about you?" I asked.

"Nothing worth worrying about, though I'm sure there's a deck of Old Maid cards somewhere in Oak River with my picture on one of the cards."

"Are you kidding me? They're calling you an old maid?"

"Not in so many words, but they've insinuated it."

"Oh my gosh, you're not even thirty yet."

"I'll be thirty soon enough."

I rolled my eyes. "Seriously? Don't tell me you're buying into that?"

"I already told you I'm not. I ignore them."

"You're the one who mentioned your upcoming birthday. It is a big one."

"It's more than six months away. And I'll hang out at The Bar like I do for every other birthday." She shrugged it off, but I could tell it was a bigger deal than she was ready to admit.

"Why don't we plan something fun? We can go somewhere...do something big?"

"We can have a good time here in Oak River, Jess. We don't have to go somewhere."

"I didn't mean-"

"Yeah, I know," she interrupted. "Look, I'm not having a mid-life crisis or anything, okay? I'm fine with hanging out at The Bar with my family and friends."

"All right," I told her, leaving it at that. I didn't want to argue with my sister over her not making a bigger deal out of her thirtieth birthday. Not like I could say much since I did absolutely nothing for my own thirtieth birthday. I was probably projecting my own regrets onto her anyway. It would have been nice to live vicariously through her party, but that was my issue, not hers.

"So what are you going to do about Danny?" she asked, and I sighed. I knew this was coming.

"I honestly have no idea. Sometimes when I'm with him, it's like we were never apart. Like we never had problems, got divorced...none of it. It feels like it did before everything went wrong. Other times, it feels like we're worlds apart."

"And when you're not together?"

"I get so stuck in my head about everything that went wrong. I don't know how to let it go."

"Did you ever think that maybe he's feeling the same way? Maybe he is having the same conflicts?" I shrugged. "You two really need to talk, Jess. You're still in love, it's only stubbornness keeping you apart at this point."

"It's not *only* stubbornness."

The waitress arrived with our plates and we paused our conversation, eyes wide, as the delicious mess was placed in front of us. There was meat, potatoes, and fried vegetables slathered in cheese and gravy. If it tasted as good as it smelled, I would be a happy camper.

"This is the last thing I'm going to say about it," Melissa began, and I set down the fork I'd just picked up.

"Okay, go for it."

"Some people wait their whole lives and never find *the one*. You found him, and now you have a second chance. I think you're afraid—no, I know you're afraid. And that's okay. It's life, Jess. It's scary sometimes. Just hash it out with him. Get it over with. I promise it won't be as bad as you think, that man loves you too much. Then you'll be together again and everything will be right in the world." She picked up her fork and dove into her mashed potatoes. "This shit is good," she said with a mouthful of food.

I picked up my own fork and scooped up some potatoes. *She was right*, I thought as I chewed.

And not just about the food.

30

I had no idea why I'd agreed to go fishing. I hated fishing. I hated the smell, the silence, the waiting...don't even get me started on baiting the hook or actually catching a fish and what that meant.

Actually, that was a lie. I knew why I'd agreed.

Because Danny asked me.

Damn him.

He showed up to my office looking all adorable in his khaki pants and dark green polo shirt with the high school logo over the breast pocket and *COACH* embroidered directly below it. His hands were in his pockets and he looked so shy, so nervous. He might as well have said *aw, shucks.*

I was a goner.

Of course, I couldn't have turned him down. Who could have?

I probably would have gone skydiving if he had asked me. He'd reminded me so much of the nervous boy who'd asked me out fourteen years ago.

Splash.

"What was that?" I asked, looking around the lake. The small wooden rowboat we were in rocked back and forth as I looked over one shoulder, then the other. There was a small ripple to my left, but whatever had made that splash sounded a lot bigger than whatever caused that ripple.

"I don't remember you being so squeamish last time we went fishing."

"The last time we went fishing was over ten years ago." *And I was probably trying to impress you.*

"It's like riding a bike," he teased with a smirk, and I wanted to knock that Oak River ballcap right off his head.

"There is nothing about fishing that is like riding a bike. *Nothing.*"

"Oh, come on, Jess. The reel spins, so do bike tires." He spun his reel for emphasis.

I glared at him. "Riding my bike doesn't smell, involve worms or fish-"

"I don't remember you being so cranky, either."

I sighed. He had a point. I used to be a bit more laid back about stuff like this, but I'd lost my familiarity with the great outdoors after all the years in the city. I used to go fishing with Danny all the time, and while I never actually fished, I'd lay on the dock/shore/boat and just enjoy the silence. Maybe read a book. Do homework. Daydream.

But now the silence was deafening, and I couldn't sit still. Which was a real problem since we were on a boat. A small boat that rocked with every single movement either of us made, even the little ones.

"I'm sorry. I guess I'm a little too city for this," I admitted, feeling embarrassed for being such a wet blanket about everything.

I'd be lying if I didn't at least say it was beautiful out on the lake. It was peaceful, and the surface of the water was smooth, like a mirror that perfectly reflected the overcast sky. Near the shoreline, you could see reflections of the nearby trees, too. The lake hadn't suffered from the drought the way the river had, which was a blessing for the wildlife. I hadn't spotted any of the deer I remembered seeing as a kid, but there was an orchestra of birds chirping and frogs croaking.

"It's no big deal, Jessie. I'll make a country girl out of you in no time." He winked, and I felt it ripple through my entire body. "In fact, I bet that girl is still in there, waiting for the opportunity to show herself."

I shrugged, neither confirming nor denying his claims. That, and I was afraid if I tried to speak, I'd be the one croaking.

Lightning flashed across the sky, a crack of thunder following closely behind. I almost capsized the small boat when I jumped, startled by the loud bang.

"We'd better get back," I said, stating the obvious.

Danny was already pulling in his fishing line. "Sorry," he said. "I didn't know it was supposed to rain."

"Me either," I said, running my hands up and down my arms to ward off the sudden chill. Judging by the dark clouds that were quickly approaching, it was going to be a doozy of a storm. "It just came out of nowhere."

"Yeah. We'll be back to the dock in about five minutes." Danny worked quickly to get the fishing equipment into a manageable pile, then he got the oars in the water and began to row.

I did my best to clean up the fishing stuff while he got us back to land. I tried to ignore the way his t-shirt flexed across his pecs every time he pushed back. I hadn't seen my ex-husband without a shirt in years, and fantasizing about him naked—shirtless—wasn't a very productive use of my time at the moment. I managed to bring some order to the fishing poles and lures, and let out a sigh of relief when I looked up and saw the dock quickly approaching.

Just as we pulled up to the dock, the sky opened and rain poured down on us. It was like that dock scene in *The Notebook*, and there was no sense in rushing because we couldn't possibly have gotten any more drenched than we already were. My jeans stuck to my legs like a second skin, and I was certain my pale pink t-shirt was see-through. As I caught Danny staring, I decided it definitely was.

We jumped out of the boat, and I grabbed what I could carry to his truck. He worked on pulling the boat up the dock and onto the bank. It was a rental, so he had to drag it back to the rental shack, where someone was waiting to receive it.

Moments later, we were sitting in his truck in the parking lot, soaking wet, staring out the windshield at the deluge of water.

I looked over at Danny. Water dripped off his hat, now a darker green from being saturated. He looked completely dejected, and I couldn't help but laugh.

He slowly turned his head towards me. "You think this is funny?" He asked.

I nodded. "Isn't it?"

He smiled and shook his head. "I just wanted today to be perfect."

"Then you shouldn't have taken me fishing," I told him.

At that, he laughed. "You're right."

31

"Can I make you dinner tonight?" Danny asked as he started up the truck. He turned the heater knob on high, and I sighed in appreciation as the warm air brushed over my cold skin. I hadn't realized I was shivering. The rain was icy cold.

Remembering he'd asked me a question, I glanced over at him. "What's on the menu?" I teased, since we hadn't caught any fish. Whenever he'd gone fishing in the past, he always cooked what he caught for dinner that night.

He stared out the windshield, and I watched as the shadows of the raindrops moved down his face. It made him look like a painting, an old-fashioned portrait. He *was* perfect enough to be a work of art. Always had been.

"I've got some steaks in the freezer at home. We can swing by the farm stand on the way and grab some vegetables to grill." He still wasn't looking at me. It was as though he was protecting himself from the rejection he was sure would follow.

"That sounds perfect," I told him. His eyes darted to mine, questions on the tip of his tongue. "Let's go," I said, patting the dashboard. "Just in case the farmers get it in their heads to close early due to the rain."

He popped the truck into gear and spun the tires as he drove away from the landing, spraying gravel behind him.

"In a hurry?" I asked, laughing.

"I figure I better get a move on before you change your mind."

I knew he was joking, but my shoulders still slumped. Had I been that awful to him? I knew the answer to that question. Yes, yes I had been that awful to him. Refusing to speak to him while we were married, and again now.

It was time, wasn't it?

"Danny," I started. I wasn't really sure what to say, but I guessed the beginning was as good a place as any.

"Yeah, Jess?" He quickly glanced at me, then returned his eyes to the road.

"I'm not really sure how to say everything I want to say, so just bear with me, okay?"

"Okay," he agreed.

"And don't say anything until I'm done. If you interrupt me..."

"Just say what you've got to say, Jessie." He didn't say it in an exasperating way, just encouraging.

I sighed heavily.

Here goes nothing.

I closed my eyes and spoke.

"Our infertility really messed with my head," I said. Getting those first few words out...admitting that to him...it was tough, but a relief at the same time. I knew he knew it messed me up, but I had to tell him that *I* knew it, too. "Something your mom said really resonated with me. I went through years of therapy, and a few minutes with your mom had me seeing more clearly than ever before," I laughed softly. "We never had any conflicts in our relationship when we were growing up. Everything was so easy. It was easy to fall in love with you, to stay in love with you. We excelled in school—both high school and college. We bought our first house, got our first adult jobs...all with no problems. It was wonderful. Our life was perfect. No hiccups, no roadblocks...no problems.

"Then, all of a sudden, there's this problem that's larger than life, you know? Like, how can there possibly be anything wrong when everything else was always so right? It made me question everything I ever thought I knew. I didn't trust myself. I thought I had to be wrong, that I was seeing our entire life through rose colored glasses because how could anything else be right if we couldn't make a baby? Not all women—not all *people*—can go to law school and graduate at the top of their class. But any woman who wanted to get pregnant should have been able to get pregnant. It's basic biology. Jesus...I'm not even sure I truly knew what infertility was until a few months had gone by, and I still wasn't pregnant."

Danny's grip on the steering wheel was tight, his knuckles white. I could tell not saying anything was bothering him, but I pressed on. I had to get it out.

"I was so bothered by everything, and I internalized all of it. I blamed myself. I hated myself. I was broken, dysfunctional. I was made wrong. I even had misguided anger towards my parents because they're the ones who made me, and they obviously didn't do it right because something was so very wrong. I was mad-" I sniffled, fighting back the tears. "I was mad at you, too, because you weren't broken like I was."

Danny turned in his seat to face me, then reached across the console and took my hand in his. He'd stopped the truck on the side of the road. "Look at me," he said. "You're not broken. You're not dysfunctional or made wrong. Damn it, Jessie, you are perfect. You have always been perfect to me, even when you thought you weren't."

His tone was tender, yet final. He was letting me know what he thought, *what he knew*, and that there was no sense in arguing with him. His unfailing loyalty caused me to break. I snapped like a dry twig.

"I took everything out on you," I said as I began to cry.

He leaned over the console and wrapped his arms around me, lifting me over the gear shift and onto his lap. "Baby, it's okay," he said, shushing me as he ran one of his hands over my upper back in small, soothing circles while the other hand held me tightly around the small of my back.

"It's not okay," I argued. It wasn't okay. It would never *be* okay. "What I did to you...the things I said...they were unforgivable."

He framed my face in his hands and brought my tear-filled gaze to his. He shook his head. "Nothing in love is unforgivable, Jessie. Nothing."

Then he pressed his lips against mine and kissed me. And I let him.

32

The kiss started soft and sweet, tentative almost. It had been years since I'd felt the press of his lips against mine. Felt the touch of his skin and stubble. Felt the wisps of his breath against my face.

It felt good. I felt good.

Danny tasted the seam of my lips and I opened for him. The moment our tongues met, sparks flew through my body. I was sure he felt it, too, since his hold on me tightened.

It wasn't long before the cab of his truck got hot. Condensation licked all four windows and our rain soaked, writhing bodies made the air thick. I was grinding against him, he was thrusting against me. Steamy was an understatement.

We broke apart and I leaned my forehead against his. We were both panting, our chests heaving. He breathed in my exhales, I inhaled his. We stayed there for a moment, looking straight into the other's eyes, silently asking, *What does this mean?*

Something.

Everything.

"Jessie...it's no secret how I feel about you. I love you, I've never stopped."

"But-"

"No buts, Jess. I was there at the end of our relationship. I know what happened as much as you do. It was a dark period for both of us and now it's over."

"But it's not over, Danny," I sighed. "I still can't get pregnant." This wasn't a problem that was going to get better with time or go away completely. It was permanent.

He tenderly ran his thumb across my cheek as he gazed at me with adoration. "But that chapter of our life—that pain—it's over, Jess."

"Don't you still want kids?" His dreams couldn't have changed. He'd always wanted a family—a big family.

"Of course I do," he answered, and my heart dropped to my stomach. "And if we need to adopt in order to have kids, then that's what we'll do. Jessie, I don't care how it happens, as long as it's with you. I want to be with *you* more than I want anything else. Shit happened, okay? A lot of it. But it's in the past now. If you feel like you need my forgiveness, you've got it. You've always had it. I never blamed you. Not one time. I knew you were torn up, I knew you were blaming yourself. I should have done more to help you emotionally."

"You did enough," I whispered, and he pressed a finger to my lips.

"And you were right with what you said before. We never had to deal with conflict and when we finally faced something that was bigger than us, we dealt with it poorly. But we're not over, Jessie. We were never over, I just gave you the space you thought you needed."

"We can't keep living like this, Jess." Danny sat on the edge of the white sofa, his elbows on his knees, looking across our living room at me. I didn't make eye contact. I couldn't. It had been six months since the last failed IVF, since that last day in Dr. Rowland's office, and I'd completely closed in on myself. I knew it was

only a matter of time before Danny was finished dealing with me and my crap.

It seemed that time was finally up.

"You won't talk to me. You won't look at me, and God forbid you touch me. You barely even leave the house, except for work, and you're a zombie there, too. I understand you're upset—depressed even—but don't you realize that I'm sad, too? We're supposed to be in this together, Jess. Instead, I feel like I'm all by myself. I've needed you. I've needed my wife...my best friend. I want that girl I fell in love with back. Where did she go? Huh, Jess? Where is that girl? The one that was so full of life and love? I know she's in there somewhere."

I shook my head, my empty stare focused on the black TV screen. I didn't even know who that person was anymore.

"She's in there somewhere," he said, getting up and walking over to me. He knelt down in front of me and took my hands. I still couldn't look him in the eye. "I'm talking about the girl who stole my heart in the tenth grade. The one who cheered at all my football games in that sexy little green cheer skirt with my number painted on her cheeks. The girl I lost my virginity to after homecoming junior year. My prom queen. The one I waited years for while we went to separate colleges. Jesus, Jess. If we could get through being separated for all four years of undergrad, we can get through this."

A lone tear dripped down my cheek, and I cursed myself for letting it fall. I remembered that girl he was talking about. I missed her, too. But she was gone...dead...right there with her hopes of having a family.

"Please, Jess. Please come back to me. If you still love me, if you want to try, say something. Please, Jess. Say something."

I looked into his light brown eyes for a moment...just a moment. They were glassy, like he was on the verge of tears. My big strong man...he was going to cry.

I broke him. Everything was my fault. I had to let him go. It was the right thing to go. Give him a chance to have everything he ever wanted. A family...

Yes, I had to let him go. It wasn't just the right thing to do, it was the only thing to do.

I tugged my hands out of his grasp, not missing the way his entire body wilted before I turned away and closed my eyes.

"I want a divorce."

I was left with nothing.

Nothing.

Nothing.

Nothing.

"I'm sorry I asked you for a divorce," I said, a stray tear sliding down my cheek.

He caught it with his thumb. "That was just a piece of paper, Jessie. It didn't mean anything in here." He tapped his chest, right over his heart.

This man. More tears spilled over my lids. *How could I have ever lived without him?*

"I love you," I told him. "I love you so much."

"I know, baby," he said, wiping the moisture from my face. "I know."

This time, I kissed him.

33

For our first official re-date, Danny and I attended a movie in the park.

Oak River had been doing these drive-in style events for as long as I could remember. Everyone brought chairs or blankets and found a spot in the grass in front of the huge white, canvas-wrapped board that served as an outdoor movie screen.

So, not only was I nervous about our first date, but we were coming out to the entire town at the same time. No pressure. None at all.

I wore dark jeans and a light green sweater. It was still a little warm during the days, but it would cool down once the sun set. I pulled on a pair of dark brown, knee-high boots and peeked out the front window. It was almost six, and that was when Danny had said he'd pick me up. He was taking care of dinner, and I was bringing dessert. We'd eat at the park, everyone did. I baked s'mores brownies, a recipe I'd found on Pinterest a while ago and had been waiting for a reason to make them. They were packed away in a Tupperware container, resting atop the thick blanket I'd promised Danny I would bring.

Headlights rolled across the wall; he was here.. I took a deep breath, readying myself. I didn't know why I was so nervous. It was just Danny.

I startled at the knock on my door. I hadn't expected him to get out of the truck, but I should have known he would. He wanted this to be a real first date, and on a real first date the guy would come to the girl's front door when he picked her up.

I hurried over and opened the door, smiling shyly at him. "Hi," I said. "Come in." I stepped aside as he came through the doorway. He looked delicious, and he was dressed similarly to me in dark jeans and a light grey, long-sleeved henley. His boots didn't come up to his knee, but they were dark brown, too, and were laced under his jeans.

"You look great," he said, scanning my body the same way I was scanning his.

My cheeks heated. "Thank you. You do, too."

He stuffed his hands in his pockets. "This is weird. Why is this weird?"

I laughed, glad he said something. "I don't know. It shouldn't be."

"No, it shouldn't." He took his hands out of his pockets as he walked up to me. His eyes hooded as he looked down at me. "Hi," he whispered.

"Hey," I said.

He leaned in and pressed his lips against mine. I went dizzy as he took my breath away.

"I know it's our first date," he said after he pulled away, "but I couldn't wait until the end of the night to do that."

"No worries," I told him with a smile. I didn't think I'd have been able to wait until the end of the night either, if I was being honest. And making out in front of the town during the movie didn't sound too appealing. We'd really be the talk of Oak River then. Inside the privacy of my home was just fine. My eyes rolled inwardly. We were going to give them enough to talk about tonight.

"You ready?" he asked.

"Yep." I grabbed my bag and the brownies and Danny carried the blanket. We locked up and walked out to the truck. Like the gentleman that he was, he opened my car door for me and waited until I was comfortable and buckled in my seatbelt. He rested the blanket on the floor by my feet and kissed my cheek before shutting the door, making me blush again.

I couldn't remember feeling this bashful with him in the past but I loved it. I loved how nothing felt old. Everything felt new and fresh and perfect. The butterflies were perfectly present and I knew in that moment that life with Danny would always be this way. I'd never be bored with him. Our life would always be full of life and love and surprises. Good surprises. First dates, warm kisses, and love. Always love.

"What's that look for?" Danny asked as he settled in the driver's seat.

"What look?" I asked, unsure of what he saw. Had I been making a face?

His eyes scanned my face and he shrugged. "I don't know. You look...happy, beautiful..."

"In love?" I offered.

He smiled. "That, too."

"I am," I told him, holding his gaze. I wanted him to know how certain I was about us. That I was taking this second chance seriously. "I am so in love with you." His eyes were shiny and I knew that was what he'd needed to hear.

"I love you, too." He leaned over and kissed the tip of my nose.

He started the truck and put it in gear, then reached over and took my hand. He held it all the way to the park.

***

"Coach T, who's this?"

194

Since arriving at the park, Danny had been approached by at least half a dozen high schoolers—a combination of his players and students. They were only a month into the school year, but his students already appeared to be enamored by him, maybe that had something to do with his position as coach of the very popular football team. Or maybe it because Danny was just that amazing to be around.

This particular student, who was probably one of his players judging by his bulk, was the first to directly ask Danny who I was. I was curious to see how he'd introduce me to one of his kids.

"This is the love of my life." Danny said it so matter-of-factly, my heart skipped a beat. He wrapped his arm around my shoulder, as though he knew I needed the extra support to keep from swooning. "Jessica Price. She's the new attorney in town." He looked at me, nothing but love in his eyes and I fell harder for him, if that was even possible.

"Jessie, this is Devin," he said to me. Then to Devin, he said, "When those contracts start rolling in, this is who you'll need to call. My girl is the best lawyer around."

I rolled my eyes and patted his firm belly. He was my biggest supporter. He'd used that same line with two other kids tonight.

"It's a pleasure to meet you, Devin," I said to the boy, putting out my hand to shake.

"Devin's our QB," Danny told me. "He'll be at the game Friday night."

Apparently, I was going to the game Friday night. We hadn't talked about it, but were officially a couple now, so I supposed it went without saying that I would be there to support him and his team at the games. I didn't mind. It would be like old times...me cheering for him on the sidelines. Cheering for Oak River.

We really had come full circle, hadn't we?

"The pleasure's all mine," Devin said with a wink. He took my extended hand and kissed it. The little flirt!

"All right, Casanova," Danny joked. "Get off my girl."

"Can't help it. She's hot, Coach."

Danny winked at me. "I know. Get back to your friends, Dev. I'll see you Monday."

"Later, Coach T. See ya, Miss Price."

"He's a character," I said, wrapping my arm around Danny's as we continued walking into the park. We had been stopped so many times, we weren't going to end up with a very good spot to watch the movie. I wouldn't have traded it for anything, though. Being there with Danny? It was priceless.

"Yeah, he's a good kid." Danny moved the tote bag carrying our food and blanket higher on his shoulder.

"What's it like?" He looked at me, raising an eyebrow. "Living your dream?" I specified.

His grin was lopsided, like the boy I'd fallen in love with years ago. "I'm not living it yet," he replied simply.

"What else could you possibly need?" I wondered.

He stopped at a space large enough for us to spread out a blanket and still have some distance from other movie goers. Setting the tote bag down, he faced me and took my hands in his.

"Well, for starters, I'm going to need you to marry me again."

My eyes widened as my jaw dropped. He wasn't...he couldn't be...

"And if I thought you were ready for that, I'd ask you. Relax, I'm not proposing tonight." He laughed, shaking his head.

He was smiling and his whiskey eyes were light, full of fun and mischief, so I knew he wasn't hurt that I went frigid on him when he mentioned the M word.

But...would Danny proposing be such a bad idea?

He was always it for me. When I'd agreed to re-date him, I knew this was it. I knew there was no turning back. And the ultimate end point in any relationship was marriage, wasn't it? Or at least forever? I was committed to forever with him. Did I want to marry Danny again? Without a doubt.

I wanted to marry him.

I wanted us to live together again.

I never wanted to go to sleep without his eyes being the last things I saw before I closed my own.

I wanted everything to be the way it was before it all went wrong. Things had changed, yes. We weren't the exact same people we were, but we were never better than when we were together. I wanted that feeling back. That love and comfort...the familiarity. I wanted that again.

Before I knew what I was doing, I dropped to my knees.

Danny's brow furrowed, "Are you okay?" He started to lower himself to the grass, too, but I held up a hand to stop him. "What's going on?"

"Marry me, Danny." His eyes widened as he realized what I was doing...what *I* just realized I was doing. "I know I'm a hot mess ninety percent of the time, but at least I'm hot, right?" I laughed and so did he. My eyes filled with tears as he wiped the corner of his. "I love you so much, Danny. We lost so much time because

I was being stupid, and I don't want to lose another minute. Marry me. We don't need to date. We know each other better than we know ourselves. We don't need to take the time to fall in love because we're already *in* love. We'll just end up loving each other more and who has time for all that anyway? Marry me. Let's start the rest of our lives together right now. I want to be *us* again. I want things to be what they used to. Please?"

He dropped to his knees in front of me and cupped my face in his hands. "You're such a brat, you know that?" he whispered. I nodded and we both laughed again. "Of course I'll marry you, Jessie. I love you so much. Thank you for coming back to me."

"Thank *you*," I said, smiling through my tears as he began kissing them away.

"I love you," he said, still kissing the tears on my cheeks, then my eyes, and finally my mouth.

"I love you," I said against his lips.

Cheers erupted around us, and I pulled away from him. A quick scan of the park made it clear that everyone had been watching us. They were still watching us now with smiles on their faces, clapping and hollering.

My cheeks flushed, and I tucked my head against Danny's chest. "Oh, my god." Danny laughed, and I felt the vibrations on my cheek.

I pulled away and looked into his eyes. He was happier than I'd seen him in years and I couldn't help but smile back at him.

The crowd began chanting "kiss, kiss, kiss." Danny wrapped his arms around me and pressed his lips against mine. He kept it chaste...he had students in the audience, after all. It was enough to get the crowd going again. Damn small town.

We broke apart and smiled at one another, my forehead pressed against his. Everything was going to be just fine.

34

My engagement ring glittered in the lights of the stadium as I sat front row for Oak River High's football game. They were currently killing the other team, a nearby rival. It was also Homecoming weekend, so the stadium was packed with Oak River alumni.

One blissful week had passed since my proposal in the park. Danny still had my original engagement ring, and he gave it to me later that night when we went back to the farm. He said a few proposal worthy things himself. I cried as he slid it on my finger, and then, like he had in the park, he kissed every single one of those tears away.

The cottage was still my home, but I had spent most nights over the past week at the farm with him. Once I officially moved in, I'd probably rent or sell the cottage. I wasn't in a rush though, and it was kind of nice to be able to escape into the cottage during the day when I needed a break from the four small walls of my office. Maybe I'd just keep it.

The stadium vibrated with stomping feet and raucous noise as Oak River scored another touchdown. I rose to my feet, clapping and whooping. I sat between Melissa and Michael—all of us wearing Oak River green—and we celebrated with smiles and high fives. Bryan and Karla had left at half-time to put the kids to bed.

Every so often, Danny would look over his shoulder at me and wink, but his focus stayed on the game, as it should. He was such a great coach. It was reflected in the way his players gave him their complete attention. They looked up to him with admiration and respect. I was always proud of him, but seeing him in his element on that field was something else. My pride skyrocketed right along with the fireworks the town set off at the end of the game when the scoreboard read *Home 35, Guest 0.*

As the stands emptied, Michael and Melissa hugged me goodbye. We were due to have a Sunday dinner at my parents' house that weekend, and it would be the first where Danny and I attended as a couple. Melissa cackled at my expression of discomfort as she reminded me of that fact.

"Mom and Dad are thrilled," Michael said, kissing my cheek before he followed behind Melissa.

I hadn't seen my parents all week. I wasn't avoiding them, I was just very busy. I had appointments with clients every day, many of which were new and required new documents to be drawn up rather than the usual edits and updates. I was actually surprised my mother hadn't made an appointment to come see me at the office, that wasn't outside the realm of possibility. She'd done far worse things with the right motivation. I imagined she was giving me space, not wanting to spook me.

The truth was, I felt solid. For the first time in years, I was comfortable in my own skin. I was happy. No, happy wasn't a strong enough word. I was...jubilant, tickled pink, blissful, delighted...

I couldn't stop smiling. I was living my best life...with Danny again. Everything was out in the open and all was forgiven. We were starting fresh. It was perfect.

I sighed happily as I moved with the crowd out to the parking lot. I waved and said hello to a few people here and there. Danny was in the locker room with the team and would meet me in the lot when he was finished giving his pep talk and spending time with any of the players or crew who needed him.

I reached one of the massive light poles in the parking lot and rested against it as I people watched. Oak River's homecoming queen was laughing near the concession stand with members of her court. Her hunter green dress reminded me of the dress I'd worn when I held that same title. It had been tradition that the queen's dress be the school's colors. I was glad to see that hadn't changed.

I was tempted to pull up the hood on my sweatshirt to ward off the cold air. The temperature had turned fall crisp over the last week, particularly at night, which was just one of the many reasons spending the evenings with Danny had been so wonderful. He kept me warm.

Speaking of Danny. I watched as he emerged from the tunnel, smiling as he chatted with one of the assistant coaches. He'd introduced me to the guy, but I couldn't remember his name so I hung back watching my man. I smiled as he fist-bumped a couple of the players, and I smiled even deeper when he spotted me and gave me a small wave, holding up one finger for me to wait for him. I nodded and just watched him, still in his element talking to his team and the coaching staff. He loved this so much. And I loved him.

His attention tore away from his conversation, and he looked to his left, out into a different part of the parking lot from where I was. I tried to follow his gaze, but saw nothing.

"Da-da" a little girl screamed.

I saw her then, a quick flash of hunter green in between two parked cars. She was little, so small that I couldn't see her above the hoods and trunks of the vehicles in the lot.

I hoped she had a parent with her, that she wouldn't get hit by a car running by herself in the busy lot. Her path was leading her straight to Danny and the other coach, maybe she belonged to him.

"Da-da," the girl called again, and I watched as she ran right up to Danny—my fiancé, Danny—and he lifted her off the ground like she was weightless.

I stared in shock as he wrapped his arms around her, smiling at her precious little face and kissing her cheeks before holding her close and spinning her around in dizzying circles.

I told myself that watching them spin in circles was why I felt nauseous.

I told myself that the cold air was why I felt numb.

I wanted to tell myself I was seeing things and that was why my heart was breaking.

35

My breath came out in short little gasps as the tightness in my chest took over. Pressure built up behind my eyes as they began to sting.

Da-da.

Danny had a child. He had a *child,* and he never said a word.

I watched as he continued to embrace the little girl, spinning her in those circles. It was as if they were in their own little world, smiling at one another and laughing. A world I wasn't privy to.

I'd seen enough.

I turned my back before the first tear fell. I wasn't going to cause myself anymore pain by continuing to watch the two of them together.

I'd come so far...too far.

We were going to get married. How could he have not told me?

As I walked to my car on the other side of the lot, I wondered how I was going to survive losing Danny a second time. The first time was terrible, but he'd moved out. He left, and I didn't have to see him on a regular basis. The city was big enough to allow you to live in the same place as an ex and never run into him. This time it was different. This was *Oak River*. We couldn't coexist in Oak River and not run into each other.

Did he think I would never find out? That he could keep it from me? What was he thinking?

He was never the problem, the evil little voice said, reminding me that I was the reason he and I couldn't have children.

Damn it. I'd worked so hard to keep her quiet. *Don't let her get to you*, Jess.

I continued to stomp my way to my car, feeling the pressure deepening in my chest and my head and knowing the dam was about to burst.

Stupid emotions. Moments like this made me long for the days of feeling nothing at all.

I unlocked my convertible and slid inside just as the first tear fell.

Drop.

I buckled my seatbelt and started the engine.

Drop.

Checked the mirrors.

Drop.

Reverse gear.

Drop.

I backed out of my parking space, put the car in drive, and tried like hell not to peel out of the parking lot. I failed.

Drop.

I pressed the button on my steering wheel to activate the Bluetooth connection to my phone. "Call Dr. Todd," I spoke into the silence.

The phone line rang four times before his voicemail picked up. I disconnected the call.

What the hell had I been planning to say anyway?

Hi Dr. Todd, it's been a few months since we've spoken and, even though I last told you I was doing great, I'm still pretty screwed up! I saw my ex-husband-slash-current-fiancé with his daughter and completely lost my shit.

I laughed out loud at myself. *Grow a backbone, Jessica. You can't go crawling back to your shrink whenever something doesn't go your way.*

But wasn't it completely legitimate for me to feel *something* about this situation? He was keeping the fact that he had a *child* from me. He's the one who was dishonest, not me. Regardless of our past, I had every right to be upset with him because of our *present*. We were trying to build something...have a fresh start. I kept nothing from him. Nothing at all. And he hid this.

After everything we went through...

No wonder he was so okay with us getting back together. He already had the family I couldn't give him.

I pulled into my driveway and turned off the car. I couldn't even remember making all the turns to get to my house and that scared the hell out of me. I needed to clear my head, and I knew just who to call for help.

***

"Are you going to share with the rest of the class?" Melissa asked, looking amused.

At least I thought it was Melissa. There were two of them, and I didn't remember my mother having twins. I closed one eye. Ok, it *was* Melissa. Just one Melissa. She was twirling a little, but she was there. I didn't remember her being a dancer either. Oh well.

"Men are stupid," I slurred, setting down my empty glass on the table. The glass shattered on the floor, sending small shards of glass all over my kitchen floor. *I guess I missed the table.*

"I guess you did," Mikey said, sighing heavily as he stood from the small kitchen table and disappeared down the hallway.

Had I said that out loud?

My eyes returned to Melissa. "Do you think he's mad at me?" I asked, watching my brother disappear down the short hall of my cottage.

She shook her head. "Definitely not. He's just worried about you, Jess. You call us up and say you want to have a few drinks. No problem. But we show up and you've already had like seven drinks, so obviously something is wrong, but you won't tell us what it is. Plus," she eyed my bag in the corner where I'd dropped it, "your bag has been buzzing the entire night."

"I'm not a very good sister, am I?"

Melissa scrunched her eyebrows together. "Why would you say that?"

"I left and got so preoccupied with school, then work, then trying to have a baby, then my emo self...why do you guys even want to hang out with me? I suck."

"Okay, you're cut off." Michael swooped in from behind me like a vulture and picked up the bottle of rum that had somehow found its way into my hand.

"Buzz off, vulture. Give me back my rum."

"No, Jack Sparrow. We've catered to your little pity party long enough. You're going to start talking or we'll use other tactics to get it out of you."

I rolled my eyes. *This guy.* "I don't even have a bulletin board, so I'm not afraid of your tacks."

Melissa and Mikey shared a look, I think they rolled their eyes at me, but I wasn't sure. Things were a bit blurry.

"I could always tickle it out of you," Melissa suggested.

"How old are we? Twelve? Grow up," I told her. She had the pokiest little fingers. I secretly hoped she'd act her age.

Melissa poked my side.

"Knock it off!" I said, nearly falling off my chair to get away from her.

Mikey poked me from the other side.

"What the heck?" I glared at him. He'd never participated in the tickle torture before.

Then Melissa pounced.

"I'm going to *pee*! Stop!" I squealed and squirmed, trying to buck Melissa off me.

"Tell me what I want to know and I'll stop." Melissa ordered.

"Not happening." I'd stand my ground.

Melissa dug her pointy little fingers into my side, under my arms, and behind my knee. I was squirming and squealing. And that was before Mikey went for the soles of my feet. The jerk.

Melissa and Mikey laughed at me and with me. I had to admit, the sounds I was making were pretty impressive and could have easily landed me a job doing sound effects for a barnyard cartoon. Snorts and all.

I was laughing and crying and laughing...until I was just crying and crying and crying.

"I think we broke her," Melissa whispered.

"Nah, I think she was already broken when we got here." Mikey was so perceptive. So perceptive, that Mikey.

My little brother and sister held me as I cried myself to sleep, mourning the loss of my new-old relationship.

36

"Wakey wakey," Melissa's voice was soft as she sat on the bed beside me.

How did I end up in my bed?

Last thing I remembered was being in the kitchen with the rum. Then Mikey took it away. And they tickled me, the little shits.

I cracked open one eye, then immediately shut it.

"Danny's here," Melissa said, and both of my eyes shot open.

"Why?" I glared at her.

"Are you serious? He was blowing up your phone last night and finally showed up after you passed out. He's been here ever since. You're mad at him? I thought you guys were past all that nonsense, Jess."

"He has a kid, Melissa. A daughter. He didn't tell me."

Melissa reared back like I slapped her. "What?"

"He has a daughter, Mel. I saw him with her last night."

The picture of the two of them under the parking lot lights last night flashed into my mind again, and my eyes filled with tears.

"Jess," Melissa said, a look of realization dawning, "I think you need to talk to Danny. This isn't what you think."

"It's exactly what I think," I yelled. Why did I have to defend myself? "I know what I saw."

"Sure, you know what you saw, Jess. But you interpreted it incorrectly. That's not his daughter. It's his niece." With one last look at me, she walked out of the room.

His niece?

How could that be? Dean didn't have any kids. I'd been in Oak River long enough that I would have run into them. Or he would have mentioned a daughter when he was working on my house. But wouldn't he have mentioned a niece? Wouldn't Danny had mentioned a niece?

Darcy.

It's a shame what she put that family through over the years. Wasn't that what Mrs. Blakeney had said in my office weeks ago?

I sat up in my bed, the quick motion making my head hurt.

Did Darcy have a child?

My bedroom door creaked open, and I looked up to see Danny standing in the doorway. He looked like he hadn't slept at all, and he probably hadn't.

I didn't know what to say. I didn't know how to explain my behavior, but luckily I didn't have to.

"The little girl you saw me with last night...that was my niece. Darcy's daughter. She calls me *Da-da* because she can't say Danny yet. She calls Dean *De-de*."

I closed my eyes, feeling like a complete asshole.

The bed sank under Danny's weight, and I opened my eyes again. His were sad now. "What are we going to do about this, Jess? You can't keep shutting down, shutting me out, whenever you freak out over something. Not to mention, how could you possibly think I'd keep something as big as having a child from you?"

I shook my head. "I don't know. I panicked. I immediately jumped to the worst possible conclusion because how could there have been a more reasonable one? I couldn't think of any better reason why you would have kept her from me unless the reason was one that would hurt me."

"I hadn't told you about Darcy and Chloe— that's her name—because I wanted to see where your head was first. Chloe is my niece, and I love her, and I was afraid that my sister's accidental pregnancy would make you hate her."

My mouth dropped open. "I could never-"

"I didn't know that, Jess. I remember conversations we had years ago when we were trying to get pregnant. I remember you saying it wasn't fair that there were so many unplanned pregnancies, and we were two people who wanted a baby so badly, but couldn't have one. That's all I could think of from the moment I found out Darcy was pregnant."

God, I remembered saying that. I remembered thinking that. Hell, sometimes I even still thought that. It *wasn't* fair, but that didn't mean I hated the mother or the child. It only ever made me hate *myself* more. It always made it seem like the entire female population functioned so much better than I did.

"I hated *me*, Danny. I never hated them," I confessed.

"I didn't know, Jess. You never really talked to me about that stuff. About how you were really feeling. I was worried about it, so I figured I'd feel you out. Darcy lives in California, so I didn't think they'd ever just show up like they did. Darcy came for homecoming, which is completely random, but that's irrelevant. I still should have told you."

"And I shouldn't have assumed the worst. I just couldn't imagine an innocent explanation to why a little girl was calling you that. Calling you Da-da. It freaked me out."

"I'm sorry I kept it from you. I was trying to protect you. To protect us. I don't want to lose you again."

"You won't lose me," I promised him. "I will learn to talk to you instead of hiding from you."

"And I will give you a little more credit going forward. You're a strong woman, Jess. I love you," he said, brushing his fingertips down my cheek.

I leaned into his soothing touch. "I love you, too."

He held me against him, and I heard him sniff. "How much did you drink last night?"

I groaned. "Too much."

He shook his head. "We need to find you some healthy outlets for your emotions."

"Like what, carrots?" I cringed at the thought of eating carrots anytime I got upset.

Danny gave me a funny look. "No, not carrots. Something like running." This time I gave *him* a funny look. "Or coloring or something."

"Okay, I'll lay off the sauce."

He laughed softly and held me tighter. "You can have a drink if you want, I just don't want you using it to self-medicate. I can think of other ways for you to do that." He winked and my entire body heated at the possibilities.

213

"I like the sound of that," I whispered, climbing into his lap.

"Yeah, not now," he laughed. "You smell like a brewery."

"Hey, now," I said, playfully slapping his chest. "All right. I'm going to take a shower."

"Good," he said, laying back on my bed as I stood up.

"Is Melissa still here?" I asked as I pulled open my dresser drawers to find some comfortable clothes to change into after my shower.

"Nah, she said to tell you she'll see you tomorrow at your parents."

"Yeah, Sunday dinner," I said, deciding on gray sweatpants and a worn out college t-shirt. I turned around and froze.

Danny hadn't spent any time in my cottage bedroom before today, and seeing him there, lying on my bed, hands behind his head and feet stretched out, with those whiskey colored walls in the background caused me to pause. The sight was so familiar, yet so new and different. I'd seen him in this exact position at our old home hundreds of times.

"You okay?" he asked.

"Perfect," I told him as I pulled my t-shirt over my head.

He stared unabashedly at me with so much heat in his eyes. I stripped off my shorts and kicked them towards the hamper basket in the corner of my room. Danny licked his lips and I smirked.

"Want to wash my back?" I asked as I turned around, giving him a full view of my back side as I walked to the bathroom.

He was off the bed and on his feet faster than I could blink.

Under the hot spray, his hands roamed my body as the water sluiced over my skin, and I thanked every deity I'd ever heard of that Danny and I had found our way back to one another.

Finally.

***

"Jess, can you pass the potatoes?" I handed the steaming bowl of mashed potatoes across the table to Bryan. "Thanks."

"You're welcome," I said, taking the gravy from Danny. Our eyes met and we shared a quick, sweet smile. Being there felt so normal, and I was glad we could still be so comfortable with each other, despite the years we missed.

Mom didn't miss our little exchange, neither did Dad. They both smiled at me and Danny. Mom's smile was a little watery. She was so happy to have "her kids" back together again, or so she said no less than ten times in the last hour.

"What's your plan with the boys for the rest of the season, Dan?" My father asked. The guys all paid attention to his response about his team and the playoffs, but I tuned it out, thinking more along the lines of wedding plans.

Danny and I had spoken last night...pillow talk...and decided eloping would be best. We weren't sure when or where, but we wanted to do something quick and meaningful, and then take a nice vacation somewhere together...a second honeymoon.

"Jess got her first online client," Danny said, sharing something I'd told him the night before.

"That's great, Jess," Karla said. Everyone else followed suit, congratulating me for expanding my practice.

"Thanks, guys. I'm looking forward to having more work. Mr. Smith's practice might have had the right pace for him, but I need a little bit more. Even if it means virtually consulting on contracts."

As I took a sip of my wine, my father clinked his fork against his glass and stood up. "I'd just like to say a little something. It's been a long time since we've had a complete, Price family dinner."

I looked down, an old, familiar feeling of guilt moving through me. Danny put his arm around my shoulder and pulled me into his side. Instantly, my racing thoughts and feelings calmed. He knew just when I needed him.

Dad raised his glass. "I'd like to formally welcome Jess and Danny back home, back to our table." I wiped a tear, raising my glass with my free hand. "Welcome back to the family, Dan."

"Thanks, Stewart." The adults all tapped glasses, and Danny got up and gave my father a hug.

I was right behind him, feeling like a little kid again in my father's embrace. "Thanks, Dad."

"We're so happy you're home," he said as he held me. "And we're so happy the two of you found your way back to each other."

Still leaning against my Dad, I turned to look at the rest of the family. Mom and Danny were standing in front of one another, my mom's hands on Danny's cheeks as they quietly spoke. Melissa and Karla were filling in the kids on what their grandfather's announcement was about, while Michael and Bryan were finishing their food, seemingly oblivious to the activities around them.

"I'm happy, too, Dad."

Epilogue

Two years later

"Jessica!" I called as I walked into the house, dropping my keys into the handmade bowl on the heart-shaped table just inside the front door. It was late, later than I usually got home but practice ran over. Our rivalry game was that week, and the team was putting in one hundred and ten percent. I had a great group of kids this year, but I said that every year. They were dedicated.

"Out here," she called. It sounded like her voice was coming from the backyard.

As I made my way through the house, the echo of my sneakers on the hardwood floor reminded me that I'd better take them off before Jess saw me. My wife hated it when I wore shoes in the house, particularly after working out in the yard or on the field.

My wife.

It may have been round two for us, but I never got tired of calling Jessica my wife. We'd just celebrated another year of marriage, making it six years total. We remarried on what would have been our ten-year anniversary, choosing to count our cumulative years together rather than starting back at one. Neither one of us really cared to dwell on the years we spent apart. We were together again, and that was all that mattered.

As I passed the mantle over the fireplace, I glanced at our side-by-side wedding photos. In the first, Jessica was beautiful in her puffy white princess gown. In the second, she was even more beautiful in a form-fitting ivory lace dress. I looked the same in each photo—wearing a black tux and looking down at Jessica like she hung the moon and all the stars. She was looking at me the same way.

"Jess," I called again as I walked out of the house to the backyard, passing underneath the 'happily ever after' sign Jess had hung above the door, the same one from our first home that she'd secretly kept all those years.

"Over here."

From my spot on our back deck, I looked across the wide expanse of the lawn and saw her sitting on the swing I'd hung from the large maple tree in our backyard. Her back was to me and I'd bet she'd been watching the sunset, the exact reason I'd put the swing in that place. I glanced at the sky, a beautiful pink reminding me of the sand at the beach in Bermuda where we'd taken our second honeymoon.

"Hey, baby," I said as I came up behind her. I wrapped my arms around her from behind and kissed her warm cheek. I felt her cheek rise under my lips from her smile.

"Hi, handsome," she said.

"I got a phone call today," I said, kissing along her jawline and down her neck.

She giggled—I loved that sound. "Oh yeah," she said, tilting her head and giving me her neck. "Who called you?"

"Andrea."

Jessica straightened up and twisted her body in the swing so she was facing me. "Yeah?" There was so much hope in her eyes. Hope and caution.

"Yeah," I said, nodding. "It's happening, baby."

"It is?"

"We're going to be parents," I told her, pulling out my cell phone and showing her the picture of the tiny baby girl we'd just gotten the approval to adopt through an international agency.

"She's beautiful," Jessica said with tears in her eyes as her finger hovered over the image on the screen.

"There's more," I said, swiping my finger across the screen so another image popped up. "She's got a big brother."

Jessica's eyes widened as she looked from the phone screen to me and back again. "A brother?"

"Maksym," I told her. "Maksym and Sofia." They were from the Ukraine.

"They're beautiful," she said, not taking her eyes off the screen. She took the phone from me and moved between the two images for several minutes. Tears spilled down her cheeks, but I didn't dare interrupt this moment for her...seeing her babies for the first time. My girl was becoming a mother right before my very eyes, even if it wasn't in the most conventional of ways.

I waited ten years for this moment. More than that, if I was being honest. I'd known I wanted a family with this woman the moment I met her as kids and we played house and school and whatever other ridiculously girly games she'd talked me into because I would have done absolutely anything for her.

I still would.

She stared at the pictures for a few moments longer before I broke the perfect silence. "Say something, baby."

She looked into my eyes and hers were brighter than I'd ever seen them.

"I love you, Danny. So damn much. Thank you for this. Thank you for giving me a family."

I smiled before I leaned in and kissed her, pressing my forehead against hers.

Everything was going to be okay.

And they lived happily ever after...the end.

Playlist

I'm a rock girl. Most people who know me know that about me. I love me some hard rock and heavy metal, but for some reason, country music is what inspired the heck out of me to finish off this story. These are some of the tracks I listened to while writing *Say Something*. I listened to a whole lot more, but these are the ones that I felt held some kind of connection to Jessica and Danny's story. In no particular order, enjoy!

Born To Love You - LANCO
Break Up In The End - Cole Swindell
In Case You Didn't Know - Brett Young
Kiss Tomorrow Goodbye - Luke Bryan
Take Back Home Girl - Chris Lane
featuring Tori Kelly
Kiss Somebody - Morgan Evans
Stay - Florida Georgia Line
Unforgettable - Thomas Rhett
Hometown Girl - Josh Turner
Hooked - Dylan Scott
Mercy - Brett Young
Small Town Boy - Dustin Lynch
Last Shot - Kip Moore
What Ifs - Kane Brown
You Make It Easy - Jason Aldean
Come Over - Kenny Chesney
What Do You Want - Jerrod Neimann
Made For You - Jake Owen
Red On A Rose - Alan Jackson

Acknowledgements

This section is always the most difficult to write because I'm always afraid I'll leave someone out. This book was hard to write. It was an idea that I had, based on personal experiences and feelings, but I wasn't quite ready for it. One day, I saw a pre-made book cover and knew it belonged to this story. So I bought it and saved it until I was ready, and I was ready sooner than I thought. I think it was because I had that cover burning a hole in my Google drive. So thank you, Marisa-Rose Wesley, for the beautiful cover that gave me the motivation I needed to get this story out. Thank you to my editor, Aimee. I enjoy working with you and I appreciate having a Shoulder Aimee to help me through editing. You were one of my rocks during my infertility experience and continue to be a great friend today. Thank you to my proofreader and BFF, Natasha. You are like my right arm and I'd be lost without you. So glad I get to spend this release day with you! To my betas, you're all amazing. I appreciate your ongoing support and feedback. My reader group – Jennifer's Chapter Chicks – you're all amazing. Thank you for reading my stories. To all the readers, bloggers, and authors who helped promote *Say Something*, thank you. I am so proud to be part of the indie book community. We rock!! To my family and friends, thank you for your ongoing love and support. To the PPGs. You all know who you are. You held me up when I was so far down, and I'll be eternally grateful to each and every one of you. And last, but certainly not least, to Brad. I love you. Thank you for being you. <3

About the Author

Jennifer was born and raised on Long Island, in New York. She relocated to South Carolina in 2002, where she met the love of her life. They got married and live their happily ever after just outside of Charleston with their fur-kid, a spoiled rat terrier named Daisy. When she's not reading or writing, she works as a behavior technician practicing ABA therapy, and is a graduate student, pursuing a degree in psychology. Jennifer is a breast cancer survivor, and she enjoys amateur photography, travelling, and music...it's a bonus when she can combine all three. She independently published her debut novel, *Our Moon (JACT 1)*, in June 2015.

Connect with Me

Email: jennifer@jenniferlallenauthor.com
Website: www.jenniferlallenauthor.com
Facebook: www.facebook.com/jallenauthor
Twitter: https://twitter.com/AuthorJenniferA
Mailing List: http://eepurl.com/b4LjgD

Books by Jennifer L. Allen

JACT Series
Our Moon (JACT 1)
Hearts in the Sand (JACT 2)
Wildflowers (JACT 2.5)

Second Chances Series
Change of Heart (Second Chances 1)
Right Place, Right Time (Second Chances 2)

Gravity Series
Force: A Prequel to the Gravity Series
(previously published in the Get Rocked! in
Vegas Box Set)

Boulder Blizzard Series
Christmas Interference: A Novella
(previously published in Christmas in the City
Anthology)

Standalone
Here Without You